THE
WORLD'S
ONE HUNDRED
BEST SHORT STORIES

VOLUME FIVE
DRAMA

THE
WORLD'S
ONE HUNDRED
BEST SHORT STORIES

[IN TEN VOLUMES]

GRANT OVERTON
EDITOR · IN · CHIEF

VOLUME FIVE
DRAMA

FUNK & WAGNALLS COMPANY
NEW YORK AND LONDON

CONTENTS

THE WORLD'S 100 BEST
SHORT STORIES

THE RETURN OF THE TIDE

By Kathleen Norris

Annie Callahan Curley, bumping her young son Matt ahead of her with a guiding knee, clutching her four-year-old Helen firmly by a pulpy hand, pushing the perambulator that contained—along with the bread and the canned corn and the graham flour—the plump body of Frank Curley, seventeen months old, and managing at one and the same time to grip with firm, thin, worn fingers her flat pocketbook, encountered in Haley's Market none other than her sister, Mary Callahan Keane, a bride of four months.

It was a sweet, sharp, sunshiny morning in November; the little Curleys were well-wrapped, and the tips of their microscopic noses were wet and red. Annie wore her thick old coat, and pretty, dainty Mary the smart homespun cape with the fur collar that had been a part of her trousseau. The market was full of glancing sunlight and clean color; the cash-registers rang and clattered, and clerks dashed about busily, brushing their way without apology between loitering women, and snatching at cabbages and boxes of crackers.

7

Mary and Annie smiled in simple pleasure as they met. Mary's first little dainty housekeeping rooms were but three blocks from Annie's overrun little household, after all, and since the Curleys had come back to Annie's home town the sisters saw each other almost daily. But it was pleasant to meet here, as Mary immediately said, grown-up, you know, and married, and buying things for their husbands to eat!

Mary plumped Helen unceremoniously into the foot of Baby Frank's coach with the freedom of familiar aunthood, and Helen squirmed herself somehow into comparative comfort upon the packages and cans.

"Hush up, Matt!" said Mary then, without heat, to the seven-year-old boy. "Here, what do you want, for the love of Pete!" she added to the child, as she opened her pretty, well-filled purse. "Half a pound, please!" she said imperiously to the salesman, indicating a great opened hogshead of mixed sweet crackers beside her.

Matt's steady "Will you, Mother—will you, Mother—will you, Mother?" died away into silence behind a toothless grin as he began the attack upon a pink-coated cocoanut confection, and Annie, after a perfunctory murmur of "What do you *say*, lover?" settled herself happily, half-supported against the counter, for a chat with Mary. She kept the coach moving gently to and fro, the length of her arm's reach, as they talked.

"Did you see Ma to-day, Mary?" she began.

"I was just in there. She wanted me to send her some pork, for beans," Mary said, instantly portentous. "I think she looks *terrible!*" she added, solemnly, blinking her suddenly misted eyes.

Annie's glance at once became grave, and she sighed.

"I think she looks terrible!" she said, drearily. "Frank thinks she looks something terrible," she went on, thoughtfully. "She's getting awful—old," she said, faintly stressing the last word to express something for which her vocabulary was inadequate.

"She's terribly lonely, maybe," Mary suggested, troubled and perplexed.

"Well, she has Marty, and Clark hasn't been gone but a month!" Annie answered, in the same tone. "Don't give him the frosted ones," she added, to Matt, wiping a pink smear from Frank's soft, shapeless mouth; "give him that graham one! Take Sister over there to those boxes, Matt, the way the baby won't see you eating them! I thought maybe I'd stop there— at Ma's, I mean—with the children, going home, and give them their lunch there," she finished mildly, to Mary.

Now Mary, and her brother Jim's wife Ida, in a recent conference concerning Ma's welfare, had decided that Annie was too easily inclined to walk in upon Ma, with her children, and impose upon Ma's hospitality for luncheon. It meant building a fire in the kitchen stove, and it meant an exhausting amount of cutting and buttering of bread, and tying of bibs, and wiping of little mouths. Of course Ma adored it, there was that to be said for it, and she and her oldest daughter could apparently have talked on comfortably for days or months as pleasantly as for hours at a time, but Ma was not as young as she once had been, and Ida and Mary, one a bride and the other the mother of but one small child, were apt to be a little hard in their judgment of Annie.

But Mary was haunted this morning by the thought of Ma, as she had just left her, moping solitary and quiet about the kitchen, and it occurred to her, brisk and radiant herself in bridal garments, and in the sweet

sunshine, that Annie's tribe, to-day, might do actual
good by lunching with "Gogga." Mary herself had her
marketing to do, and then she and another young wife,
a neighbor, were going into the big city to see a "fil-
lum." Loretta Walsh, as Loretta Keating, had been
Mary's intimate friend since Third-Grade days; they
would buy a package of dye this afternoon, two chocolate malted milks, four hair nets, and a half-pound of
wrapped taffies, a stuffed pickled cucumber in a delicacy
shop for Billy Walsh, who loved this particular relish,
and a pair of new garters for Daniel Keane, whose old
ones, Mary said, were a disgrace.

The entertainment, and this shopping, would con-
sume four happy hours: the young women would
wander, giggling, and with linked arms, through the
greatest shopping district of the whole world: up Sixth
Avenue, across Thirty-fourth Street. They would de-
bate at windows, follow passing costumes with critical
eyes, discuss bobbed hair and the length of skirts. And
they would reach home wearied and sated with the
sheer joy and thrill of living, just in time to serve
bridal dinners of chops, Saratoga potatoes, and cream-
puffs from the bakery, to the enslaved Billy and Dan.

It was many years since Annie Curley had been free
for any such idle, aimless enjoyment. The Curleys,
unsuccessful in Albany, had recently returned to town,
to be no more successful here. And Mary, suddenly
smitten by the thought, and of the chains that these
three small, exacting children must be, and perhaps
half-consciously touched by the paleness and plainness
of Annie's face, stamped already with the first shadow
of a new responsibility, said affectionately:

"Do go in, An'! Ma gets so lonely lately. I—I
wish I could. But I sorta promised Loretta——"

"Oh, go on with Loretta, while you can!" Annie said, heartily, with a smile on her motherly face. "It won't be forever. How do you feel, anyway, Mary?" she asked shrewdly.

Mary flushed and laughed, half-resentful and half-amused.

"Oh, for Heaven's sake, Annie! You and Ida are cautions! Every time you look at me you're sizing me up!" she said, impatiently. "This morning Ma was having her coffee when I went in, and when I said I didn't want any—for I was just from my own breakfast—you'd die at the look she gave me! 'Does the smell of it make you sick, Mary?' she says. 'No, Ma,' I says, in a regular yell, 'I love it. The smell of coffee is a regular perfume to me! I'll tell you when there's any news,' I says, 'and until then I wish to goodness you and Annie would lay off me!' "

Annie laughed indulgently and deprecatingly as the trim and pretty Mary vigorously delivered her protest, with her pink cheeks growing pinker under her snug veil, and her square slim shoulders erect under the brown cape.

"I know," she said, apologetically. "But there's no happiness like it, Mary," she reminded her sister, as she settled Frank, made Helen comfortable, and prepared to go upon her way.

"So I see!" Mary said, significantly and satirically. Annie only laughed again. She would not have given up one kiss in the damp back of young Frank's neck for all the shopping, for all the shows, in Christendom. But there was no possible way of persuading Mary of that; no need, yet awhile, thought Annie, in her motherly fashion.

"But say, lissen, Annie," Mary said, suddenly, just

as they were about to part. This was the customary
proceeding; they would now exchange, after their first
farewells, the real news of the day, if news there were.
"Lissen, Annie," said Mary. "Dan and I were talking
about Christmas this morning. What are you and
Frank planning to do?"

"I wish we could have you all, and Josie and John,
too," Annie said, wistfully. "But I don't know how I
could manage it——"

"You'd be crazy to try it!" Mary assured her,
heartily. "And I suppose poor Ida won't have a
family dinner," she said, thoughtfully. Ida, their
brother's wife, had lost a little son, not much more than
a year before, a tragedy that had plunged all the different branches of the family into bitter sorrow.

The Jim Callahans had Cecelia left, to be sure, and a
lovely little girl she was. But for Jim, the adored one
brother of the family, to lose his splendid little
Francis—Francis who was so clever, and so handsome,
and so generally adored—was a frightful blow to them
all. Francis's mother had been rendered almost chron-
ically melancholy, and Ma Callahan had suddenly
seemed to collapse into age and grief under the sorrow.
For months the women of the family brooded upon
all the horrors of the child's last hours, upon the
funeral and the days preceding the funeral, when he
lay so quiet and so beautiful in his white serge First
Communion suit, looking, with his dropped long black
lashes upon his rosy, handsome little face, like an
angel already.

The months had brought some little comfort to Ida:
she knew now that St. Valentine's Day would find
another baby in her arms. She would go to Annie's
cluttered, crowded flat, and sit for hours with Annie's

fat, healthy baby in her lap, and altho down Ida's cheeks would pour the quiet tears that four-year-old Cecelia wiped away again and again, yet she grew quieter, and the very weeping seemed to relieve her.

And then, in August, there was Mary's wedding, and all the excitement attendant upon the establishment of one more little home in the world, and Josie and John Concannon had come down from Albany, with their four-year-old Rose Agnes, in her white coat with the beaver collar, and there had been much felicity and innocent mirth among them all.

But Jim Callahan never for an instant forgot his boy, and there was a certain new and weary droop to his big shoulders, and a pathetic, seeking look in his eyes, in these days, and Ma Callahan grieved so for her grandson that her daughters sometimes told each other fearfully that "it'd be the death of her yet."

She liked best to sit in her kitchen, that clean and empty and quiet kitchen that had been the theater for so many young tragedies and comedies, so much eager young living, and talk of the past and especially of little Francis, with Annie, or Kate Oliver, or some other member of the family. If chance supplied a fresh listener, some quiet little neighborhood mother with awed eyes, and with a baby tugging at her breast, then Mrs. Callahan would review the whole terrible thing from beginning to end.

If only she had spoke to Ida, when she did be noticing that little Francis looked as pale as a curd!—she would lament. That was "the Tuesday," mind you, and they didn't have the doctor to him until "the Thursday" night. The hands on him was as cold as ice, but then he'd been out with all the Sodality boys, and sure, she thought it was no more than that he was tired.

"Well, then, and on the Wednesday morning," the tale ran, "he stepped in on his way to school. And he had a great way with him, that he'd be getting out of you what he wanted, mind you, and him as grave as a Bishop! 'Gogga,' he says, holding up the little bold face of him the way I could kiss him, and me hands in the dough——"

And Mrs. Callahan's tears would begin to fall fast, remembering the beaming little face that was so soon to vanish from among the other beloved faces, and the busy little plotting, loving heart that in a few brief days was to lie cold and still. Annie and Mary came to dread those recitals; their anxious eyes, perhaps tear-filled in turn, would watch her while she rocked, sighed, wept, and recalled the agonizing details one after another.

Last Christmas had been terrible, and now here was another Christmas upon them, and it behooved Mary, the bride, and Ida, for the sake of her unborn child, and Annie, always a tower of strength and help, to make it as easy as possible, perhaps even happy, for Ma and Jim. The Concannons might come down, and they would all be together; anyway, they must brace up, the sisters decided, and make the best of the situation.

"Ma's simply not fit to have all the excitement and fuss!" Annie offered, dubiously. "And Ida expecting, you couldn't ask it of her; it'd kill her!"

"No, but this is what I was thinking," Mary said. "Ida and Jim have got a spare room, and we have, too. Now if Josie and John came down to them, quietly, you know, and not exciting Ma in the least, and then if I took Rose Agnes at our house—Dan'd love it, he's cracked about kids, anyway, and then if we got a frozen pudding made at the Tea Shop—they're perfectly delicious——"

"Say, Mary, I think that would be wonderful!" Annie said, radiantly. "Matt, just be Mother's patient darling boy—just a minute—Mother's coming right along——" she interpolated, to her impatient eldest. "I'll tell you what I can do," she said, eagerly; "Frank's sure to win one of those twenty-pound turkeys in the raffle at the club, he always does; and the Cottle Works always give their married employees turkeys, anyway, and I'll roast the two turkeys and bring them right over. Frank'll manage that! We won't say one word to Ma——"

"Ida'll make the cran-bry," Mary added. "And vegetables are nothing—the canned ones are just as good if you leave them in a cullender for two hours or more——"

"Well, hear the old housekeeper!" Annie laughed, in fond pride. Mary flushed happily and consciously.

"Well, they are!" she said. 'We could have a soup—the bean soup and the tomato mixed is simply grand. Loretta had it the other night—it was grand, *really!* And then the turkeys and fixings, and then dessert—that's oceans. I'll tell you what we'll do—we won't say one word to Ma until Christmas Day itself; you ask her to your house, and say it's going to be just your own family. And then, about eleven, we'll walk in on her——"

"I'll give the children a late breakfast—or maybe Kate would keep them for me until about one," Annie interrupted, enthusiastically, "because we don't want any noise or racket. And then we'll clean them all up,

and we'll all go, Ida and Cecelia and Jim, and John and
Josie with Rose Agnes, and Frank and me with our
three, and you and Dan. That'll be—that'll be twelve—
thirteen, with Ma. We can't sit down thirteen——"

She paused, and Mary frowned thoughtfully.

"Marty!" she remembered suddenly. The small
derelict that Mrs. Callahan had adopted years before
had been visiting Josie in Albany, and had been de-
layed for weeks, instead of the originally intended
days, by measles. "He and Rose Agnes will be all over
the measles by then," Mary announced, in satisfaction, "and Josie will bring him down. Ma's always
happier when she has Marty, anyway. And she has
lots of china, and scads of napkins; you and I'll just
put her in a chair, and keep everything serene, and
Ida and Josie can heat things up, and then all the
children will come in! And afterward, we'll just let
her talk to Jim quietly, and we'll clean up every last
spoon and send the children home, and have a real
good visit with her alone."

Annie was so excited, and so pleased by this plan,
and Mary so inspired to perfect it by fresh details, that
but for the enraged impatience of young Matthew Curley to get home, and the sudden whimpering of little
Frankie for his noontide baked potato and top-milk,
the sisters might easily have spent another hour, or
two hours, in rapturous communion. But Annie's
motherly compunction suddenly awoke, and Mary remembered her engagement with Loretta, and they
hastily parted, both still wrapped delightedly in the
thought of the Christmas conspiracy, even while Mary
raced home to drop her parcels and run for the sub-
way, and Annie, hungry, tired, and confused, engineered
her hampered way toward Ma's.

Of this loving little maneuver to give Ma Callahan all the joy of a Christmas reunion without the nervous anxiety and effort of arranging it, Frank, Dan, and Jim approved, each in his separate individual way. Dan exultantly kissed his wife, and said that he'd bet it was all her idea, and that she was a wonder.

Frank, with whom affairs at the Iron Works were not going well, and who was still worried about the bills from Annie's last illness, also kissed his wife, more soberly, and gave her the proud and tender smile she loved, and told her that nothing but blessings could follow a daughter that was as good as she was. And mind you, if he didn't win a turkey this year— but all the fellows thought he had the luck of the old boy himself about it!—she was to buy a big turkey, and pay for it. The children were all well, God bless them, and the only thing now was that eighty-two to Doc Pocock and they'd squeeze that out very easy, without scrimping on the Christmas turkey, said Frank.

Annie's whole soul went out to him in a wave of love and gratitude. They had just been bringing themselves to face, in the last few days, the probability of the coming of a fifth child. Annie had lost one baby, before birth, but there were three hungry, dirty, wet, exacting, restless, wakeful little Curleys in the six-room apartment now, and Frank had money worries, and the cost of everything necessary to safe and comfortable living was what he called "crool." Only he and Annie knew what it all meant: the utter madness of fatigue and worry and work, the mountain of tiny cares that crushed all the sweetness out of living for awhile. Sleepless nights, stumbling errands about the darkened rooms in the chill of midnight, sour bottles, wash-tubs piled high with dirty, worn, buttonless little garments, and always the whining, crying, fretful little voices. Annie knew every detail of it. And yet she had said to Frank, two or three nights before: "Let's have the first thing we say of him be 'God bless him,' Frank!" and she kissed her husband now, when his patient goodness could go on beyond her and the children, and extend to Ma, with a rush of love and confidence that no hardship and struggle could do anything but deepen.

"Easier than poor Ida, Frank!" she said, thinking of Francis's little grave piled with a second winter's snows. And Frank, drawing his own splendid boy toward him, reverently nodded.

Jim approved the Christmas plan with his new sad, quiet smile. If Ida could stand it, he said questioningly. Ida, tears rushing to her eyes, said bravely yes, that she would like it, and that Cecelia would love being with Gogga and all the children. Ida had never been a pretty woman, but she had filled out in her seven married years, and she did not wear her glasses so much, and she was the most domestic of all the young wives in the family. She got into Jim's lap, and Cecelia, the exquisite and blue-eyed four-year-old, with a flyaway mop of pure gold hair, clambered in, too, and they all clung together.

"You won't mind it, Jim?" Ida pleaded, remembering last Christmas, when she and Ma and Jim had all battled through a bitter snowstorm to the new little grave in the Flushing cemetery, and that Ma had had a chill after it, and that Annie and her young baby had come over to Ma's and how they all had gotten to crying in the Christmas evening.

"No, my darling," he answered, gravely, with a deep patient sigh.

"It isn't like a regular family Christmas," Ida said, "because we really have to think of your mother, Jim, and save her, now. It's all going to be managed very quietly, with no strain and no confusion, and she'll not have any of the trouble or fuss at all. And next Christmas—Jim, dear," she went on, timidly, "next Christmas *will* be happier, won't it, Jim? You will feel happier, won't you, especially if it's a little boy that God sends us?"

"I think maybe another girl would be better—I don't know, it seems like a boy would put him out of his place," Jim said, thickly but steadily. "I guess we'd love the little feller—but he wouldn't be my Francis. Two years since we gave him his coaster——"

And he got up slowly, placing her and Cecelia gently in the chair he left, and went heavily into the kitchen, like an old man, and she heard the outer door shut. Ida, burying her wet face in Cecilia's mop, wept her heart out. If only—if only—there didn't ever have to be a Christmas again!

Launched in a whirl of enthusiasm, the conspiracy for Ma's happiness was destined to encounter disheartening squalls. The chief of these was the attitude of Ma herself to the once-welcome holiday season. She appeared to be totally indifferent to all talk of Christmas trees, presents, family reunion. Discouraged, but not daunted, Annie duly asked Ma to have a quiet Christmas dinner with Frank and herself and the children. Ma accepted lifelessly; poor Ida and Jim would be going to the graveyard, she opined.

"Maybe Josie and John'll be down, and bring Marty home," Mary hinted one day, really alarmed at her mother's apathy. Marty, Mrs. Callahan's adopted child, was the very apple of her eye.

"I hope they won't then," her mother answered, despondently and firmly. "Why they'd bring the poor child down to a forlorn old woman like me, when he's safe and happy with them, the dear knows! I'll come over and have a bite of dinner with Annie, but I hope the none of you'll go to any fuss with turkey and ice-cream! Poor Jim's heart is broke out of him without his boy, and Mary just married; who knows but what Dan would want to take her to his folks in Wilkes-Barre for Christmas Day!"

"We went there Thanksgiving, Ma darling," Mary said, tenderly and patiently. "Ah, please do try to cheer up for Christmas, dear!" she pleaded.

"I don't know why I would," her mother faltered, with watering eyes. And she froze their hearts within them by adding, in an undertone: "Maybe I'm tired. Maybe it's that I'm getting to the end of me road!"

Josie raised other objections almost as depressing. Josie was the middle daughter, most prosperously married to a physician in Albany, and with a beautiful home, and a motor-car, and a general promise of rising to social heights that would have paralyzed her own Irish grandfather with sheer terror.

She wrote that altho she and John had not seen Ma for six months they were sure that the big family party at home would be too much for her. She was failing; there was no question about it. And that raft of children, and all the chatter and excitement might kill her. Besides, Ida was expecting in a few weeks, and poor Jim was simply crushed after little Francis's death, and it would be an awful struggle for Annie to roast turkeys, and get the children clean, and all the rest of it.

Now why wouldn't it be better to give the children a nice early dinner, say at four o'clock on Christmas Day, and then all go into New York and have a fine restaurant dinner, with John and herself as hosts? John thought that would be the only sensible thing to do, and then he and she could take the ten-o'clock train back to Albany, and the others go home when they pleased. She would leave Rose Agnes with John's mother in that case, as the excitement of the long trip and the full day would be too much for the child——

Mary, Ida, and Annie raged when they had this letter. Josie had been suspected of a certain airy sense of superiority more than once; now they were sure that she was completely spoiled. Egged on by the others, Annie wrote her a firmly reproachful letter, assuring Ida and Mary that if Jo wanted to get her feelings hurt, why, they simply would have to be hurt, that was all.

But Jo replied meekly and submissively, as it happened, and so reestablished herself in their hearts. Her letter, three days before Christmas, brought comfort and courage to them all. She would come, of course, and bring Rose Agnes and Marty, and they'd all go in upon Ma at noon on Christmas Day and help cook dinner, and have a perfectly gorgeous time.

By this time a threatened change in the management of the Iron Works was, however, unduly worrying Frank Curley, and Annie was sure that her suspicions as to her own condition were justified, and Jim had pleaded off from attending the Christmas party: he'd be all right, he said, he'd just take a long walk. Ida, who knew where the long walk would lead him, cried herself to sleep, on the eve of Christmas Eve, with disappointment, and Annie felt ready to die with utter discouragement and heartache.

But Christmas Eve came in with a whirling, glorious snowstorm, and in the cold, sunless morning Josie, looking stunning in her furs, and her big John, and little dancing Marty, and Rose Agnes, all arrived, with a carload of packages and a thousand cold and laughing kisses. Annie's kitchen became a riot of voices and shouts; Ida and Cecelia came over, and after work, that afternoon, Jim stopped in, and kissed his sister, and talked to blue-eyed little Rose Agnes in his kind, sorrowful voice. And Ma never dreamed—Ma hadn't the slightest notion—Ma was as innocent as an angel! they told each other exultingly, over and over.

"And she told me yesterday," Mary said, "that she thought she'd never let another Christmas go by again without making an effort. She said she wished she'd asked Jo to send Marty down! She said she didn't think she'd live to see another Christmas——"

"For Heaven's sakes!" Josie exclaimed, turning from one face to another in distress. "That doesn't sound like Ma! Is she as blue as all that?"

"Oh, my!" Annie and Ida and Mary all ejaculated together, shaking their heads in mournful triumph. "You wouldn't know her, Jo. She's just—well, she's a different woman!"

Josie made no answer in words, but her eyes watered with a sort of angry and incredulous pain. The girls were exaggerating, she thought resentfully. She had come from her trim little home, her nicely managed little establishment, with its clean Danish girl in the kitchen, and its delightful order and prosperity, and everything here in the old environment looked shabby, shiftless, unnecessarily ugly, to her.

After the first flush of meeting Annie she had noted the general poverty and plainness of Annie's house, and the worn, patient courage of Annie's soul and body. She had at once suspected Annie's secret, and the fact itself annoyed her, as well as the fact that Annie did not tell her about it. Another baby! Jo thought, despairingly, her intolerance springing from sheer affection for and loyalty to Annie, and yet hurting Annie far more than mere indifference would have done.

Then Jim hurt her, too, for Josie adored her only brother, and the thought that this wretched attempt at merry-making to-morrow was to be made without him cut her to the heart. No, he said quietly, to her coaxing, he'd a little rather not try it to-morrow. They weren't to worry about him; they weren't to think about him at all. He'd be all right. He saw Ma all the time, he went in every other day to see her, and she would understand.

To put a final touch upon Josie's discouragement, young Marty, who had been visiting her, developed a thick, painful throat this evening. If Marty had mumps, then of course Rose Agnes would have mumps! And probably the whole Curley nursery would catch them, and perhaps poor Ida, who never had had them, and who was in no condition to fight any illness. Josie wished heartily that they had never attempted this ridiculous party!

John and Frank and Jim and Danny, warned not to go near Ma, went out, after dinner, to see old friends in the neighborhood. But the women sat about in Annie's crowded parlor, putting the finishing touches to Christmas dolls and beribboned doilies, and talking in continually sinking and saddening voices of family matters. And Josie was conscious only of a desire to scream at them all that they were a helpless, stupid, fearful lot, and then grab her baby and rush back to her own home, where women read the backs of the magazine, and men were not afraid of losing jobs. Frank Curley had nothing to be afraid of—he was a master-mechanic, after all, and there were other iron works in the world. To have Annie—who had been so pretty and so neat, sighing here, and wiping her eyes, and biting threads——!

Marty, asleep upon a lounge, woke up fretful. His throat hurt! The women looked at each other, appalled.

"Try him on a teaspoonful of vinegar, Jo!" Annie whispered, as they threaded their way between the filled beds in the dark bedroom. "My goodness, I wish we could ask Ma!"

They were to reach Ma's just at noon the next day; by eleven o'clock they were all tired to the breaking point. Annie had dragged herself to early Mass, sick and dizzy, had come back to roast turkey and boil potatoes even while every fiber of her being was in revolt at the mere smell of food. She spoke to the children gently, screamed at them, and spoke gently and apologetically again. Frank did his best, buttoning clean rompers wrongly and misunderstanding directions.

Marty, Matt, Helen, and even the baby, were reminded that they must make no noise at Gogga's; Gogga was not well. To Ida's Cecelia the directions were repeated, and to Josie's exquisite Rose Agnes. Over and over again the sisters arranged their plans: the turkeys would be in Ma's oven, and the ice-cream on Ma's back porch, before she fairly knew what was afoot.

Through a sweet, clean Christmas noon, of dazzling snow and bright sunshine, with bells ringing, and holiday joy abroad in every red-painted coaster and consciously worn fur collar, they presently trooped to the old house. By this time the children were in wild spirits, and John and Dan laughing together, and even to Annie's lifeless cheek an unwonted happy flush had sprung.

The gate creaked; they were up the path, they were at the door. How well they knew the rubbed dirty space about the bell, and the pencilled "Roslyn 369" that some impatient messenger had scrawled there!

A long delay; then Ma at last, with an amazed almost truculent look in her handsome face, and one big foot bare. She had been soaking her foot in a bucket of warm water; she looked as if her privacy had been somewhat outraged.

"Well, whatever——!" she said, drily. "I thought I was to go to Annie! And you're down, Josie? Forevermore! Take his cap off, Frank, for the Lord's sake, the way he won't have his ribbons all chewed to nothing on you! It's a wonder you wouldn't let a body know—I've a taste of stew in the icebox, and that's all——"

Even their greetings, their resolute laughter and comment, could not quite carry it, could not make the ensuing hours a success. Even when the kitchen stove, and the stove in the parlor, were roaring hot, and the presents had been given, and the table enlarged and set, and the cranberry sauce divided into glass saucers, there was a consciousness of something forced in their hilarity, and something missing to their felicity.

The women chattered courageously; Ma wasn't to do anything, but they did everything gaily as they moved to and fro. Annie's face blazed, she looked her pretty self again with her red cheeks and shining eyes; she had pinned on a great, stiff white apron, and put a cluster of red berries into her lifeless, meekly lopped hair. Mary was irresistible, and Josie merry and affectionate, and full of stories and gossip that were new. Ida sat near her mother-in-law, a little breathless, and more than a little apprehensive. She kept running over the months, upon nervous finger-tips; June to February came out nine, and over and over. And yet she did have a queerish feeling.

The men helped clumsily, eagerly, or stood about, large and awkward, smoking. Any little topic of conversation that they could keep moving they followed with passionate seriousness. Also they spoke frequently to the children, who were beginning to feel restless and hungry as the clock struck two.

It was Ma who was responsible for all this discomfort. Ma, who in old times had been the animated, garrulous, loving, dictatorial heart of all their groups, was oddly changed and aged to-day. She received them magisterially, with a certain aloof dignity. She watched them, she listened, she considered her answers. There was a stiffness, a sort of tacit disapproval in her manner, that made them all uneasy.

This had been home to her three girls once. But nobody felt at home here to-day. The irresistible currents of life had drawn them away, one by one, and they were alien here. The depth and passion of their mother's love had only been able to show itself, after all, in endless little services, in the daily intimacies of coffee cups and ironing-board; now those services were no longer needed, and those intimacies had been long interrupted, and she felt her children to be strangers.

More than that, her only son was absent, roaming the snowy world desolate and alone, his big heart aching for his son. And when she remembered Jim, Mrs. Callahan's heroic struggle to seem natural and happy died away in ashes and despair. It was a fine Christmas Day whatever, she reflected, without a sight or sound of the lad!

"Do you know, I think she would have liked it better if we'd put the whole job up to her," Mary murmured, despondently, to Annie, in a moment of privacy. "I believe she'd have liked to do it—I'm afraid it's kind of hurt her, our taking it out of her hands!"

"I think so, too," Josie agreed, stricken. "She acts so funny. She just answers 'yes' and 'no'—not a bit like Ma!"

"Well, we'll just have to go on with it," Annie answered, sighing. For the dinner was in the actual process of dishing up. Annie was on her knees at the oven; the two great turkeys smoked deliciously, the mashed potatoes was a little Fujiyama of white and gold.

From an epicurean standpoint nothing could have excelled the meal. Ma herself had never roasted more wonderful turkeys, Josie's biscuit was perfection, there were gravy and jelly and dressing and corn pudding for a multitude. The children stuffed, passed plates, and stuffed anew; their elders showed only slightly inferior appetites.

And yet there was a singular heaviness in the air. Ida secretly mourned for her absent Jim, and counted the months from June to February with a sinking heart. Annie filled Frank's plate with the choicest bits of everything, timidly watching for his smile. Josie talked gallantly, altho a certain feverish heaviness upon the part of little Rose Agnes was making her heart stand still with terror. She reminded Mary later that, after all, it was Dan's first Christmas with the family—it would be a nice thing to have him think that they were all deaf mutes! Ma ate, complimented the cooks punctiliously, addressed herself principally to her grand children. Once she remarked that little Francis had been with them at Christmas-time two years ago, and wondered aloud who would go next.

Failure. The family dinner was an absolute failure. Annie could have wept, thinking of the money and time and effort that had been wasted to force this wretched affair into being. The men were heavy, dull, and in the way, when the ice-cream and cake were finished at three o'clock, and the children were ubiquitous and quarrelsome. Their grandmother roused herself only apathetically to reprimand them. She said that if Jim had gone to the cemetery he'd likely get his death, too, a day like this.

The sun had gone behind leaden clouds, and a cold raw wind was blowing over the sunless snow. Josie was practically and briskly preparing the six children for a good half-hour's play out-of-doors when her husband, in his capacity as doctor, interfered. It would be dangerous, flushed and tired and excited as they were, to send them out so late in the winter afternoon, he said. No, Rose Agnes positively should not go. No, it was not safe.

John was always so gentle and kind that Josie felt

his tacit reproof like a blow. Tears were in her eyes as she wiped glasses and spoons and knives and plates and plates and plates at the old, familiar sink. Ida was ready for tears, too; it was a strange Christmas Day without Jim. And Annie was exhausted almost to the point of joining them; she felt as if it were physically impossible for her to get home this afternoon, and get Frank a cup of tea, and tumble the children into beds. She fairly ached with fatigue.

"Put your coat on, Frank dear, and step up toward the cemetery, and see if maybe you can't get hold of Jim, and tell him how bad Ma feels!" she whispered, over the hot clean knives. "Don't worry, darling!" she added, kissing him tenderly as he turned to obey.

But as the patient, shabby shoulders disappeared, in the stiff, thick old coat, she felt a dry ache of tears in her throat, and she ran after him to kiss him again.

Mary was secretly distressed, too, for all her noisy, mirthless chatter, because Dan wanted to get away for the five-twelve run of "The Price of Her Lie." It was opening at the Plaza to-day, and Dan knew the fellow in the ticket-office, who had said that he would always take care of Dan in the matter of tickets.

To Mary it did not seem quite decent to run away from the family on Christmas Day. Ma had never let them go to shows on Sunday night, and she would surely suspect, and perhaps anger Dan with a sharp word on the subject. So she managed to keep away from Dan's neighborhood, and Dan appreciated it perfectly, and resented it.

"Ma," Josie asked, anxiously, "how do you know when it's mumps?"

"I suppose by taking them into a hospital, and cutting something out of them!" her mother replied,

witheringly, and altho Josie joined in the laugh that
followed, it was not without a glance half-pitying and
half-pleading to Ma.

The shabby old rooms were very hot and heavy with
food odors now, and in frightful disorder. Christmas
toys were mingled in among the mussy plates and
tumbled napkins, and the steamed windows were
marked by dirty little sticky fingers.

It was Matt Curley, masticating an immense hard
chocolate candy, and lounging in youthful *ennui* against
one of these windows, who said suddenly, over the
general hubbub of the dining room:

"Oh, gee, look—it's a drunk. Oo, no, it's not—
they're bringing him in—it's a man that's been
killed——"

"God save us, what's the child talking about?"
Annie muttered, as she and Mary and Josie flew to
the window. "O God be good to us! *God be good to
us!*" she said, in a deep hard tone that rang through
the room.

One moment, peaceful dishwashing and cheerful
Christmas disorder, and the next moment—*this!* This
view of the familiar yard, the gate blocked with snow,
the bare lilacs rattling in a bleak wind under a sullen
sky. And the men—strange, silent, huddling men, in
their heavy, worn overcoats, bringing something hide-
ous, heart-stopping in—bringing something in——

There were screams, and the stamping of quick feet,
and the children were pushed aside. A bitter draft
of icy out-of-door air clove through the thick, food-
scented rooms. Big muddy feet tramped in; the cluttered table was shoved aside; they laid Frank Curley
down upon the dining-room lounge. To the half-circle

of pallid-faced, terrified women some man, gruffly and awkwardly, spoke.

"It was Cottle's car—poor Frank was up by the Iron Works—he'd asked some fellow there had he seen Jim Callahan. It was Cottle's fault—there was a cop right there, and he said so!"

"Oh God help us—God preserve us——!" the women whispered, their eyes upon the helpless, sodden lump that was Frank. A great gasp and shudder went through the craning group when Mary, her young face ashen, gently eased the crushed head upon a crimson velvet cushion, and Frank moaned.

Suddenly Annie came through the press; Annie with the freckles showing upon her pale, strained face, and the years of patient motherhood stamped upon her flat, thin body; Annie, with work-worn hands and her sweet trembling mouth.

She sank quietly upon her knees beside him, and took the torn, discolored hand that had been roughly rolled in mud and snow in her own hand, and her thin cheek rested upon his rich disordered hair. Over and over again the motherly voice said softly, breathlessly:

"Frank—my sweetheart! My own true husband——!"

She looked bewilderedly at John Concannon as he gently put her aside. Josie, crying, was holding a basin of water; Mary, ashen-faced, was behind the couch, supporting the stained, muddy head. In the background there was a huddle of terrified faces. Annie saw her baby boy, in his high-chair, with his big new ball in his fingers, and with a piteous trembling of his little mouth.

She caught him to her flat breast, stumbled into the kitchen, Matt and Helen clinging to her blindly, and found herself and her children suddenly caught in her mother's great arms.

"Come, now, darlin'," said the familiar voice, with all its old heartening vitality and ring, "Annie—be a woman, dear! He'll want to see you the minute he opens his eyes. It's only a bad fall, dear! Take courage to yourself——"

"Ma——" It was poor Ida, forgotten in the last few moments of uproar, but staggering with pain and clinging tightly to the big comforting shoulder. "Ma— I don't know that I can get home——"

Mrs. Callahan, distracted in spite of herself, fixed alert eyes upon her son's wife. With Ida writhing and helpless, and Annie sunk in a stupor of agony upon a chair, her children pale and frightened about her, a sudden energy and courage almost youthful seemed to descend like a visible mantle upon their mother.

"The dear Lord stand by!" she said, richly and heartily concerned. "Don't you have a moment of worry, Ida, dear, you'll be fine! Matt, take a handful of wood, and run up to Aunt Josie's old room, and make a grand little fire in the stove," she commanded. "Get hold of Uncle Dan, Helen, and tell him Gogga wants him. I'll send Mary upstairs with you, dear, and you just take everything easy—it'll all be over very quick, this time, I told you so a month ago! John's here, when you need him, and as soon as poor Frank feels better—sit where you are, Annie, and keep the baby in your arms—you poor girl, you. I'll go in and find out how things are going——"

Brisk, capable, resourceful, she stepped from her kitchen with the old, erect step of long ago. She immediately assumed control of everything that was passing in the dining room; somehow the onlookers scattered, and the children disappeared, and the door was closed. And by degrees, with here a little help from Josie, and there a little more from Mary, the big table was cleared, and pushed empty against a wall, and order succeeded chaos.

Outside, the dark, brooding Christmas Day moved heavily to twilight. The wind, howling bleakly, ruffled the shawls and hats of frightened women, gathered whispering and glancing, in the snowy yard. Josie and Mary, and John and the strange doctor, fussed incessantly about the still unconscious and occasionally moaning Frank. Annie had the old rocker, close beside her husband, now; the baby was asleep in her lap; one of her thin, work-worn hands held Frank's hand.

Dan came back, with the nurse for Ida. John Concannon was free for a few minutes to step upstairs. And Josie waylaid him in passing, and drew him into the big bedroom next to Ida's—the bedroom that had for so long been Jim's. Would he just look at Marty and Rose Agnes? Wouldn't it be the terrible thing if this was mumps, after all?

They had a brief talk, husband and wife, and then Ma came panting up, to find Josie in frightened tears.

"Shame upon you, Josie Callahan, the way you would be weeping and lamenting over such a thing entirely!" said Ma, roundly, half-shaking and half-ambracing the terrified Josie. "Wit' poor Annie never lettin' a cry out of her—and the child smilin' up in the face of her, and his father all but dead on him——!"

"All but dead?" Josie echoed, shocked, and instantly upon her feet, her tears died. "Ma—is he so badly hurt?"

"We don't know yet, dear," said John, gently. But he slowly shook his head. Josie looked from one to the other, her lips steady, and a new look in her eyes.

"Why, mumps are nothing!" she said, quickly and reassuringly. "Rose Agnes would have to have them sometime, and I don't know where I'd rather be than here with Ma! I'll put her in one bed, Ma, and Marty in the other, and John can go back home without me when he has to go!"

"Well, now you're talking like yourself, dear, and you're a great comfort—for all you're so nervous about the child, entirely!" her mother said, in approval.

"And is Ida better, John?" Josie asked, sensibly, as she dried her eyes, and began to examine the available blankets and pillows.

"Ida?" he said, smiling a little. "You know what's happening there?"

"What!" Josie whispered, aghast. And as her look met their answering, significant glances, she turned a little pale, undecided whether to laugh or cry. "Ma—!" she faltered. And then "Ma——?"

"Well, why not? Sure, she's much more comfortable here, with the pack of us to look out for her," Mrs. Callahan said, reassuringly. "It won't be much work! I've got the turkey pretty well cut up—we'll have a big pot of stew, and a sheet of me cornbread for supper. And that'll be enough, with plenty of tea all night in case me young lady here"—she glanced toward Ida's room—"keep us all up. And please·God it'll be a healthy baby, boy or girl—for it's a little soon—and give Jim something to fill up the poor broken heart of him!"

"I'll get these youngsters to bed, and fire up the other stove," said Josie.

"Mumps, is it?" asked Mary, who had just come in, and stood, in her water-and-blood stained Christmas finery, smiling at the now consciously important Marty and Rose Agnes. "Well, never a dull moment—that's your house, Ma! Kat's come in," she added, "and she said she'd take Helen and Matt home with her, the way they wouldn't get the contagion, and Jule Mooney's here, she's got the kitchen like a pin. Dan's gone on to find Jim!"

"I'll give Jim Callahan a piece of my mind, walking off on all of us this way!" Mrs. Callahan said, heartily. Her daughters' surprised looks met; there was in them a certain deep amusement and relief. It was good to hear Ma scolding and bossing again! And Ma went downstairs with the step that had not echoed so buoyantly through the shabby old house in months. She had mourned, she had brooded, she had petted and sympathized with Jim. But there was no health in all that compared with this sturdy and vigorous resentment!

"You'd think it would kill her," Mary whispered, following.

"Well, there's no help for it, anyway!" Josie said.

At seven o'clock that evening Jim Callahan came quietly downstairs and into his mother's kitchen. He looked weary, but there was a look of utter peace upon the handsome dark face, and his Irish blue eyes were dark with happy tears under the black crest of hair.

His mother, in an iron-gray calico, with a great stiff white apron tied about her waist and a knitted pink-and-gray shawl about her shoulders, was seated, in a big rocker, by the range. A good fire was going, and now she rose, opened the oven door, and placed before her son a great plate of smoking, delicious food.

Jim looked at her a little timidly, her expression was

magnificently stern. But it was wonderful to him to have Ma her old, scolding, busy self again, managing the whole crowd of them with this scornful, brisk superiority. He brushed his face against her arm affectionately and said boyishly:

"Go on, Ma. Jump me, and have it over!"

"A big, strong feller like you," his mother began, readily, and witheringly, "stravaging the streets on Christmas Day, like a Turk that has no home, and poor Ida and the little one-een laying up there—and might be dying like poor Roso Costello herself, and you maybe at the minute buying yourself a cigar!"

"I didn't buy myself any cigars to-day," poor Jim said, meekly. "I—I'm ashamed of myself, Ma. But somehow—being Christmas—and thinking of him—the square little friendly feller he was——"

"Well, now you've got another boy to worry the heart out of you, and have measles, and sauce you back, and play hookey, and smoke cigarets on you, the way you done on me!" his mother said, roundly and unemotionally. "Did Kate give you a peek at the child?"

"She brought him in. Ide and I had a look at him, and then Ide went to sleep," Jim said, grinning, and then openly wiping his suddenly wet eyes. "He seems a fine little feller. I—I am grateful, Ma. I'm not going to let little Francis's going spoil everything for Ide any more. I'm going to take her and the children out for picnics—the way we've always done—I know I've made it harder. I'm sorry, Ma. I don't know what got into me. But it'll all be different now. You'll see!"

"I wouldn't wonder if the Lord would take the others, now, if there's any more of this running off

from your good wife and breaking her heart on her!"
his mother warned him, sternly.

"Yes, I know, Ma. You'll see, Ma!"

"Well, I hope I will!" Mrs. Callahan said, briefly.
"Fine goings on for the man of the family," she muttered, "and now," she added, suddenly, with a glance
at the closed dining-room door, and in a lowered voice:
"Now maybe with Annie—poor girl!——"

Jim's face shadowed.

"I know it!" he said, quickly. "It makes me
ashamed that I ever thought of my own trouble. Ma,
we'll stand by her if poor Frank don't pull through,
won't we, Ma?"

"She'll have her mother, and her mother's home, and
we'll do what we can," his mother said, with a sudden
quiver of her handsome mouth.

"Any change, Ma?" And Jim glanced in turn at
the dining-room door.

His mother compressed her mouth, narrowed her
eyes, and slowly shook her head. Mary and Dan,
returning from a trip to their own home, where Cecelia
and Helen and Matt were established for the night,
quietly entered the kitchen, shuddering with the cold,
and powdered with the first flakes of a fresh blizzard.

"Any change, Ma?" Mary whispered. And "Any
change, Ma?" Josie, returning from a last glance at
the victims of the mumps, echoed anxiously.

"No, there's no change," their mother answered,
with a significant look. And heavily she added:
"There'll be no change. John's there, and poor Annie
sits there—she won't go to bed. We'll have to stand
by poor Annie now, ger'rls——"

"Oh, Ma, we will!" Mary and Josie cried, passionately, one on each side of her chair, on their knees, arms locked about her.

"She and her children will never want," Jim said, steadily. "Poor Frank didn't speak to me. But when she was out of the room I knelt down beside him, and I said that to him. And the look that came into his eyes—he knew what I meant! There's many a millionaire that doesn't leave his children what Frank Curley does!"

"You said the truth then," Mrs. Callahan assented, with a great sigh. And for a few minutes there was silence in the warm, orderly kitchen. Then Ma roused herself, glanced at the stove, glanced at the clock. "Well, I'm going to set me bread," she announced, rising. "With sickness in the house there's not much good in baker's stuff. Christmas—and all of us together for a little celebration—and look what's in it! May God make us resigned. Life's short for all of us!"

But in the firm, capable hand that reached for the pan, and in the bend of the straight back, and in the keen glance of the black Irish eye, there was no sign of breaking. Life and death were hovering over her house, and the future was chaos, but the years had brought back the Callahan children to Ma's guidance and Ma's service, and the heart of Agnes Callahan, little as she or any one else suspected it, was singing a song of gratitude and triumph within her breast.

A DARK-BROWN DOG

By Stephen Crane

A child was standing on a street-corner. He leaned
with one shoulder against a high board fence and
swayed the other to and fro, the while kicking carelessly at the gravel.

Sunshine beat upon the cobbles, and a lazy summer
wind raised yellow dust which trailed in clouds down
the avenue. Clattering trucks moved with indistinct-
ness through it. The child stood dreamily gazing.

After a time, a little dark-brown dog came trotting
with an intent air down the sidewalk. A short rope
was dragging from his neck. Occasionally he trod upon
the end of it and stumbled.

He stopped opposite the child, and the two regarded
each other. The dog hesitated for a moment, but
presently he made some little advances with his tail.
The child put out his hand and called him. In an
apologetic manner the dog came close, and the two
had an interchange of friendly pattings and waggles.
The dog became more enthusiastic with each moment
of the interview, until with his gleeful caperings he
threatened to overturn the child. Whereupon the child
lifted his hand and struck the dog a blow upon the
head.

This thing seemed to overpower and astonish the
little dark-brown dog, and wounded him to the heart.

(From "Men, Women and Boats," in the Modern Library;
copyright, 1924, by the Modern Library, Inc.)

He sank down in despair at the child's feet. When the blow was repeated, together with an admonition in childish sentences, he turned over upon his back, and held his paws in a peculiar manner. At the same time with his ears and his eyes he offered a small prayer to the child.

He looked so comical on his back, and holding his paws peculiarly, that the child was greatly amused and gave him little taps repeatedly, to keep him so. But the little dark-brown dog took this chastisement in the most serious way, and no doubt considered that he had committed some grave crime, for he wriggled contritely and showed his repentance in every way that was in his power. He pleaded with the child and petitioned him, and offered more prayers.

At last the child grew weary of this amusement and turned toward home. The dog was praying at the time. He lay on his back and turned his eyes upon the retreating form.

Presently he struggled to his feet and started after the child. The latter wandered in a perfunctory way toward his home, stopping at times to investigate various matters. During one of these pauses he discovered the little dark-brown dog who was following him with the air of a footpad.

The child beat his pursuer with a small stick he had found. The dog lay down and prayed until the child had finished, and resumed his journey. Then he scrambled erect and took up the pursuit again.

On the way to his home the child turned many times and beat the dog, proclaiming with childish gestures that he held him in contempt as an unimportant dog, with no value save for a moment. For being this quality of animal the dog apologized and eloquently expressed regret, but he continued stealthily to follow the child. His manner grew so very guilty that he slunk like an assassin.

When the child reached his doorstep, the dog was industriously ambling a few yards in the rear. He became so agitated with shame when he again confronted the child that he forgot the dragging rope. He tripped upon it and fell forward.

The child sat down on the step and the two had another interview. During it the dog greatly exerted himself to please the child. He performed a few gambols with such abandon that the child suddenly saw him to be a valuable thing. He made a swift, avaricious charge and seized the rope.

He dragged his captive into a hall and up many long stairways in a dark tenement. The dog made willing efforts, but he could not hobble very skilfully up the stairs because he was very small and soft, and at last the pace of the engrossed child grew so energetic that the dog became panic-stricken. In his mind he was being dragged toward a grim unknown. His eyes grew wild with the terror of it. He began to wiggle his head frantically and to brace his legs.

The child redoubled his exertions. They had a battle on the stairs. The child was victorious because he was completely absorbed in his purpose, and because the dog was very small. He dragged his acquirement to the door of his home, and finally with triumph across the threshold.

No one was in. The child sat down on the floor and made overtures to the dog. These the dog instantly accepted. He beamed with affection upon his new friend. In a short time they were firm and abiding comrades.

When the child's family appeared, they made a great row. The dog was examined and commented upon and called names. Scorn was leveled at him from all eyes, so that he became much embarrassed and drooped like a scorched plant. But the child went sturdily to the center of the floor, and, at the top of his voice, championed the dog. It happened that he was roaring protestations, with his arms clasped about the dog's neck, when the father of the family came in from work.

The parent demanded to know what the blazes they were making the kid howl for. It was explained in many words that the infernal kid wanted to introduce a disreputable dog into the family.

A family council was held. On this depended the dog's fate, but he in no way heeded, being busily engaged in chewing the end of the child's dress.

The affair was quickly ended. The father of the family, it appears, was in a particularly savage temper that evening, and when he perceived that it would amaze and anger everybody if such a dog were allowed to remain, he decided that it should be so. The child, crying softly, took his friend off to a retired part of the room to hobnob with him, while the father quelled a fierce rebellion of his wife. So it came to pass that the dog was a member of the household.

He and the child were associated together at all times save when the child slept. The child became a guardian and a friend. If the large folk kicked the dog and threw things at him, the child made loud and violent objections. Once when the child had run, protesting loudly, with tears raining down his face and his arms outstretched, to protect his friend, he had been struck in the head with a very large saucepan from the hand of his father, enraged at some seeming lack of courtesy in the dog. Ever after, the family were careful how they threw things at the dog. Moreover, the latter grew very skilful in avoiding missiles and feet. In a small room containing a stove, a table, a bureau and some chairs, he would display strategic ability of a high order, dodging, feinting and scuttling about among the furniture. He could force three or four people armed with brooms, sticks and handfuls of coal, to use all their ingenuity to get in a blow. And even when they did, it was seldom that they could do him a serious injury or leave any imprint.

But when the child was present these scenes did not occur. It came to be recognized that if the dog was molested, the child would burst into sobs, and as the child, when started, was very riotous and practically unquenchable, the dog had therein a safeguard.

However, the child could not always be near. At night, when he was asleep, his dark-brown friend would raise from some black corner a wild, wailful cry, a song of infinite loneliness and despair, that would go shuddering and sobbing among the buildings of the block and cause people to swear. At these times the singer would often be chased all over the kitchen and hit with a great variety of articles.

Sometimes, too, the child himself used to beat the dog, altho it is not known that he ever had what truly could be called a just cause. The dog always accepted these thrashings with an air of admitted guilt. He was too much of a dog to try to look to be a martyr or to plot revenge. He received the blows with deep humility, and furthermore he forgave his friend the moment the child had finished, and was ready to caress the child's hand with his little red tongue.

When misfortune came upon the child, and his trouble overwhelmed him, he would often crawl under the table and lay his small distressed head on the dog's back. The dog was ever sympathetic. It is not to be supposed that at such times he took occasion to refer to the unjust beatings his friend, when provoked, had administered to him.

He did not achieve any notable degree of intimacy with the other members of the family. He had no confidence in them, and the fear that he would express at their casual approach often exasperated them exceedingly. They used to gain a certain satisfaction in underfeeding him, but finally his friend the child grew to watch the matter with some care, and when he forgot it, the dog was often successful in secret for himself.

So the dog prospered. He developed a large bark, which came wondrously from such a small rug of a dog. He ceased to howl persistently at night. Sometimes, indeed, in his sleep, he would utter little yells, as from pain, but that occurred, no doubt, when in his dreams he encountered huge flaming dogs who threatened him direfully.

His devotion to the child grew until it was a sublime thing. He wagged at his approach; he sank down in despair at his departure. He could detect the sound of the child's step among all the noises of the neighborhood. It was like a calling voice to him.

The scene of their companionship was a kingdom governed by this terrible potentate, the child; but neither criticism nor rebellion ever lived for an instant in the heart of the one subject. Down in the mystic, hidden fields of his little dog-soul bloomed flowers of love and fidelity and perfect faith.

The child was in the habit of going on many expeditions to observe strange things in the vicinity. On these occasions his friend usually jogged aimfully along behind. Perhaps, tho, he went ahead. This necessitated his turning around every quarter-minute to make sure the child was coming. He was filled with a large idea of the importance of these journeys. He would carry himself with such an air! He was proud to be the retainer of so great a monarch.

One day, however, the father of the family got quite exceptionally drunk. He came home and held carnival with the cooking utensils, the furniture and his wife. He was in the midst of this recreation when the child, followed by the dark-brown dog, entered the room. They were returning from their voyages.

The child's practised eye instantly noted his father's state. He dived under the table, where experience had taught him was a rather safe place. The dog, lacking skill in such matters, was, of course, unaware of the true condition of affairs. He looked with interested eyes at his friend's sudden dive. He interpreted it to mean: Joyous gambol. He started to patter across the floor to join him. He was the picture of a little dark-brown dog en route to a friend.

The head of the family saw him at this moment. He gave a huge howl of joy, and knocked the dog down with a heavy coffee-pot. The dog, yelling in supreme astonishment and fear, writhed to his feet and ran for cover. The man kicked out with a ponderous foot. It caused the dog to swerve as if caught in a tide. A second blow of the coffee-pot laid him upon the floor.

Here the child, uttering loud cries, came valiantly forth like a knight. The father of the family paid no attention to these calls of the child, but advanced with glee upon the dog. Upon being knocked down twice in swift succession, the latter apparently gave up all hope of escape. He rolled over on his back and held his paws in a peculiar manner. At the same time with his eyes and his ears he offered up a small prayer.

But the father was in a mood for having fun, and it occurred to him that it would be a fine thing to throw the dog out of the window. So he reached down and, grabbing the animal by a leg, lifted him, squirming, up. He swung him two or three times hilariously about his head, and then flung him with great accuracy through the window.

The soaring dog created a surprize in the block. A woman watering plants in an opposite window gave an involuntary shout and dropped a flower-pot. A man in another window leaned perilously out to watch the flight of the dog. A woman who had been hanging out clothes in a yard began to caper wildly. Her mouth was filled with clothes-pins, but her arms gave vent to a sort of exclamation. In appearance she was like a gagged prisoner. Children ran whooping.

The dark-brown body crashed in a heap on the roof of a shed five stories below. From thence it rolled to the pavement of an alleyway.

The child in the room far above burst into a long, dirge-like cry, and toddled hastily out of the room. It took him a long time to reach the alley, because his size compelled him to go downstairs backward, one step at a time, and holding with both hands to the step above.

When they came for him later, they found him seated by the body of his dark-brown friend.

THE SILVER CRUCIFIX

By Antonio Fogazzaro

"Your coffee, milady," said the maid.

The Countess did not reply. But altho the curtains were closed, her handsome young face could be dimly discerned on the white pillow. The maid, standing tray in hand at the foot of the bed, repeated more loudly:

"Your coffee, milady."

The Countess sat up, while she yawned, with eyes still unopened, "Let in some light."

Her maid went to the window without putting down the tray, and, in turning the handle of the shutters, managed to knock over the empty cup on its saucer.

"Keep quiet!" whispered the mistress in a tone of irritation. "What is the matter with you this morning? Don't you see you are waking the baby?"

And as a matter of fact the infant was now awake and crying in its crib. The lady turned toward the child's bed, and peremptorily called out "Hush!"

This silenced her offspring at once, excepting for a few faint moans.

"Now, then, I will have my coffee," commanded the Countess. "Have you seen your master yet? Why, you are trembling all over! What is the matter with you?"

What, indeed, ailed the girl? Cup, saucer, sugar-bowl, and coffee-pot were rattling on the tray. "What is it?" repeated the Countess.

If the maid's face showed signs of alarm, no less was the mistress disturbed by doubts and fears.

"Nothing," replied the servant, still trembling.

The Countess hereupon seized her by the arm, shook it roughly, and exclaimed:

"Tell me!"

Meanwhile the pretty little head of a child of four was peering over the edge of the crib.

"It's a case," said the maid, half in tears, "it's a case of cholera."

Pale as death, the lady started up, and instinctively looked at her listening son. She jumped out of bed; by a single gesture she imposed silence on the girl, while motioning her to go into the next room. Then she darted to her child's crib.

The little fellow had begun to cry again, but his mother kissed and petted him, played and laughed with him until he forgot his woes, and stopped weeping. She pulled on her dressing-gown in great haste, and joined the servant, shutting the door behind her.

"Oh, my God, my God!" lamented the girl between her sobs, while the other woman too began to shed tears.

"Hush, for Heaven's sake! On no account must baby be frightened! What about this case—where is it?"

"Here, milady! Rosa, the steward's wife. She was taken ill at midnight."

"Heavens! And now—?"

"She is dead. She died half an hour ago."

The baby was shrilly clamoring for his mother.

"Go," said the Countess; "go in and play with him.

Keep him happy; do anything you like. Be quiet, darling!" she exclaimed. "I shall be back in a moment." Upon which she rushed to the Count's room.

The lady was blindly, insanely afraid of the cholera; nothing but her passion for her child could have been more intense than this feeling. At the first rumors of the epidemic she and her husband had fled the city, escaping to their splendid country seat—her marriage portion—in the hope that the disease would not spread thither. The place had been spared in 1836, and had even remained untouched in 1886. And now there it was, in the farmyard attached to the villa.

Disheveled and untidy, she flew into her husband's room. Before speaking she gave two violent tugs at the bellrope.

"Have you heard?" she said, with flaming eyes.

The Count, who was phlegmatically shaving his beard, turned round, inquiring, with the soapy brush in his hand: "What?"

"Don't you know about Rosa?"

"Oh, yes, I know," was his calm response.

If, in the first place, the Count had cherished some vague illusion that his wife was ignorant of Rosa's death, it now also seemed proper to reassure her by his cool demeanor. Instead, however, her ladyship's eyes shot fire, and her features were savage with anger.

"What!" she shouted, "you know, and you can think of nothing better to do than shave? What sort of man are you—what sort of father—what sort of husband?"

"Good Lord!" cried the Count, throwing up his arms.

But before the poor man, soaped up to the eyes, and wrapped round with a towel, could add another word, in came the valet. Her ladyship commanded that not a peasant from the farmyard should be admitted to the

house, and that no one should go thence to the farmyard. After this she gave orders for the coachman to
be ready within an hour; he must harness to the landau
the horses which his lordship would select.

"What are you going to do?" asked the latter, who
had recovered himself meanwhile. "Nothing rash, I
must insist."

"*Rash*—how dare you say that? I am willing to be
obedient to you in everything, but when it comes to a
question of life and death—my son's life, you understand—then I will listen to no parley from any one. I
wish to leave here at once. Order the horses, please.

The Count grew annoyed. How could matters have
come to such a pass as this? Was there any propriety
in running away after such a fashion? And then, what
about business affairs? In two days, or one day, or
maybe in twelve hours, he would be ready to start.
But not before—no. His wife, however, interrupted
him violently: "Propriety, indeed, and business! For
shame!"

"And clothes?" objected the husband. "We must
certainly take some with us. You see, we shall really
need more time."

The Countess made some contemptuous answer. She
would see to it, she assured him, that the trunks were
packed in an hour.

"But where do you expect to go?" persisted the
Count.

"To the railway station, first of all, and then wher-
ever you like. Now order the horses."

"I have had enough of this!" cried the other. "I'll
give such orders as I choose! I'll let the business
affairs go, and everything else! Your clothes, too!

The sorrels," he added, enraged, to the domestic who was standing by impassively.

The Countess dressed and did her hair with the utmost speed, at moments clasping her hands in silent prayer, distributing commands, summoning servants from various parts of the house by frantic pulls at the bell. There was running up and down stairs, banging of doors, shouting, laughing, calling out of names, suppressed swearing. All the windows facing the fatal farmyard were immediately closed. Thus the cries of the unfortunate children who had lost their mother were shut out; besides a disagreeable odor of chlorin had penetrated into the villa, and even into the Countess's room, smothering the delicate Viennese perfume she habitually used.

"Heavens!" she exclaimed angrily, "now they are doing their best to ruin everything! Pack up quickly, and get those trunks locked! This frightful smell is enough to kill one! Don't they know that chlorin has no effect? They ought to burn the things. The steward will be dismissed if any thieving goes on."

"Some things are being burnt already, milady," observed one of the maids. "The doctor is having sheets, coverlid, and mattress burnt."

"That's not enough!" snapped the Countess.

Here the Count, shaved and dressed, entered his wife's apartment. He began talking to her aside.

"What shall we do with these servants? We can't take all of them with us."

"Anything you please. Send them away. Nothing will be safe in the house if they remain. I don't want them to get the cholera, and then fumigate the rooms with that vile chlorin, and perhaps burn up some of

my best gowns. They have no respect whatever for
their masters' property, and—"

Furious at having yielded, the Count now broke in
with:

"A pretty state of things! A shame, I tell you, a
scandal, to sneak off like this!"

"That's it!" retorted the woman. "That's just how
you men always are! To appear strong and courageous
is more important to you than the life and safety of
your family. You are afraid of becoming unpopular.
Well, if you want to keep up your reputation, why
don't you send for the mayor, and present him with a
hundred lire for the cholera patients of the place?"

He thereupon suggested that he would stay at the
villa alone, and that she should go with the child.
Only he had not enough stability to carry out his own
idea.

During this conversation the trunks were being filled.
The little boy's playthings, his most expensive apparel,
prayer-books, bathing-suits, jewelry, crested note-paper,
furs, underlinen, many superfluous and few necessary
articles were thrown in helter-skelter, and the lids
closed down by sheer force. Then the Countess, followed by her spouse—who made a great show of ac-
tivity, but really accomplished nothing—hurried through
the whole house, opening drawers and cupboards, taking
a last look into them, and locking them up with their
own hands. The Count stated his opinion that it might
be advisable to partake of some refreshment before
commencing the journey.

"Yes, yes!" ironically said his consort, "we'll take
some refreshment! I'll show you what to take!"

And she drew up her husband and all the servants,
including those who were going home for a holiday,

and dosed each one with ten drops of laudanum. Her son she regaled with some chocolates.

At last the landau stood before the door. Prior to actually departing, her ladyship, who was extremely pious, withdrew to the seclusion of her bedchamber for a final prayer. Kneeling at a chair, in her tight-fitting costume of white flannel, her black, eight-button gloves reaching to the elbows, and her gold and platinum bracelets, she raised her eyes devoutly to heaven— under the overshadowing plume of her black velvet hat —and murmured a feverish supplication. Not a word did she say to God about the poor wretches who had lost their mother; nor did she ask that the cholera might spare the humble workers chained to the rich soil which had given her this house, her jewels, clothes, Viennese perfume, her education, her dignity, her husband and child, her accommodating God. Neither did she ask anything for her own person. She, who already saw herself and her family smitten down with the dread disease on the journey, offered up no prayers excepting for her son. In fact, her lips simply muttered Paters and Aves and Glorias, while her mind was altogether with the child, thinking of the fearful fate which might befall him, of the danger to his health in this precipitate journey, of his possible loss of appetite, sleep, spirits, or color. Oh, if he could but be kept unconscious of any peril or pain assailing others!

Rapidly she crossed herself, donned a long, gray cloak, and shut a window that had remained open. Before the strong morning breeze clouds were chasing across the sky, the grass was bending on the lawn, and the tall poplars were swaying in the avenue leading to the villa. But the Countess, tho brought up on family traditions, had no thought for reminiscences of her youth belonging to this country estate. She merely closed the window and went downstairs.

The mayor was conversing with his lordship by the carriage door.

"Have you just come from there?" she asked the official, and, being informed that he had come from his home, she upbraided him for not having kept off the epidemic. He excused himself with polite smiles, to which the lady confusedly replied: "Never mind, then; never mind," as she hastened her child into the vehicle.

"Did you give him the money?" she whispered to her husband as soon as she was seated beside him. He made a sign in the affirmative.

"I should like to thank her ladyship, too," began the obsequious mayor, "for the generosity with which—"

"Oh, it was nothing—nothing!" interrupted the Count, scarcely knowing what he said.

Established in the carriage, the Countess made a rapid survey of bags and boxes, coats, and shawls, umbrellas, and parasols. Her husband in the meantime turned round to see if all the luggage was in its place in the barouche, which had been fastened on behind to the landau. "But," he suddenly remarked, "what is the matter with that little boy?"

"Yes, who is that crying?" excitedly called out the Countess, leaning far out of the carriage.

"All ready!" exclaimed the peasant who had been assisting the servants with the luggage, and to whose side clung a small, ragged urchin. "Stop, can't you?" his father bade him, sharply, then repeating the words, "All ready!"

The Count, with his eye on the boy, plunged into one of his pockets. "Don't give way, my boy; you shall have a soldo all to yourself."

"Mother is ill," whined the lad sorrowfully; "mother has the cholera."

Up jumped the Countess. Her face livid and contorted, she brought down her folded sunshade across the coachman's back:

"Drive on!" she shrieked; "drive on—quick!"

The menial whipped up the horses. They began to prance, and then went off at a gallop. The mayor barely had time to leap out of the way, and his lordship to fling out a handful of coppers, which scattered on the ground at the peasant's feet. He stood motionless —while the boy continued weeping—and stared after the flashing wheels of the carriage that rolled swiftly away, whirling up the dust.

"Damn those rich pigs!" he said.

Pretending not to hear, the mayor discreetly departed.

The peasant, a man of middle age and stature, pale, meager evil-looking, and as rugged as his offspring, made the youngster pick up the coins. Then they went home together.

They inhabited, in the yard belonging to one of the Countess' farmhouses, a tumble-down, unplastered brick hovel, situated between a dung-hill and a pigsty. Before the door gaped a dark ditch, from which issued an indescribable stench, and which was bridged by a single rough plank. Upon entering, one found one's self in a dingy, unpaved sort of cavern. There was no flooring, either wood or stone, but there was an irregular brick fireplace, and in front of it the ground had been depressed by poor wretches kneeling to cook their mess of cornmeal. A wooden stair—three steps missing— conducted to the room, foul with dirt and rubbish, where father, mother, and son were wont to pass the night in a single bed. Standing by this article of furniture, one might look down into the kitchen below through the broken boards. The bed occupied the only spot not soaked by the rain that dripped from the roof.

Crouching on the floor, her head leaning against the edge of the bed, sat the peasant's cholera-stricken wife. Altho but thirty, she looked old; at twenty she had been a blooming girl, and even now preserved remnants of mild beauty. At the first glance her husband understood; he swallowed an imprecation. The child, frightened by his mother's discolored face, kept in the doorway.

"For Christ's sake, send him away," she moaned feebly. "I have the cholera; send him away. Go to your aunt's, dear. Take him away, and send me the priest."

"I'll go," said the man to her; and to the boy, motioning toward the farmyard gate, "You go to your aunt's."

From the porch of the yard he fetched an armful of straw, carried it into the kitchen, and went upstairs to his wife, who by exerting all her strength had contrived to get on the bed.

"Listen," said the man, in accents of unusual tenderness; "I am sorry, but if you die in the bed it will have to be burnt. You understand, don't you? I have brought some straw into the kitchen—a nice lot."

Too weak to answer, she made a mute signal of assent, and then a faint effort to rise from her couch. But the man took her up in his arms. By a gesture she begged him to reach first for a small silver crucifix hanging on the wall; she pressed it fervidly to her lips while her husband carried her down to the kitchen.

Here he made her as comfortable as he could on the straw, before going for the priest.

And now she, too, this poor creature lying alone like a beast in a cage on the already infected straw—she, too, before departing to an unknown world, began to pray. She prayed for the salvation of her soul, convinced that she was guilty of many sins, and tormented by her inability to remember them.

When the timid doctor, sent by the mayor, arrived, he asked in great fright whether there was any rum or marsala in the house. There was neither—so he recommended hot bricks for her stomach, put up a notice of quarantine, and left her. The priest, who knew no fear, carelessly reeled off what he termed "the usual things," obscuring the divine message with words of his own. Nevertheless, tho benighted and ignorant, the dying woman derived comfort and serenity therefrom.

His task done, the priest went. Meanwhile the husband had put a few more handfuls of straw under her back, and lit the fire to heat the bricks. His wife went on praying—less for her child than for the man whom she had pardoned so often, and who was embarked on the road to perdition. Finally, kissing the cross, her mind turned to its giver. She had received it sixteen years back, at her confirmation, from the Countess, the mistress of the splendid manor where it was a joy to live and of the wretched hovel where it was a joy to die. At that time the Countess was a young girl, and had presented the silver crucifix to the laborer's daughter at the suggestion of her mother, then mistress of the estate, a kind, gentle lady, long dead, but unforgotten by her humble tenants.

The dying woman acknowledged having thought ill

of the new mistress, of having complained sometimes, so that *her* husband had cursed because, despite repeated petition, neither roof, nor flooring, nor staircase had ever been repaired, and because the window frames had not been filled with linen panes. Feeling truly penitent, in her heart she implored forgiveness of his lordship and her ladyship; and she besought the Holy Virgin to bless them both.

At the moment when her husband placed the scorching bricks on her stomach, a spasm ran through her body, and she gave up the ghost. The man flung some straw over her blackening face, wrenched the little cross out of her hand, stuffed it into his pocket with a scowl at its small value, mumbling some customary pious sentiment the while.

But he did not say, for she did not know, and we do not know, how much good this poor woman's crucifix had done, invoked and kissed by her on so many occasions. Still less can we tell how much benefit may yet spring from that charitable thought of an old lady, descending to an innocent child, and afterward reascending as a prayer from a pure heart to the Throne of Infinite Mercy.

The same evening the servants at the villa, who had been given leave of absence during the journey of the Count and Countess, got drunk in the drawing-room on rum and marsala.

THE STICK-IN-THE-MUDS

By Rupert Hughes

A skiff went prowling along the Avon River in the unhurried English twilight that releases the sunset with reluctance and defers luxuriously the roll call of the stars.

The skiff floated low, for the man alone in it was heavy and he was in no greater haste than the northern night. Which was against the traditions, for he was an American, an American business man.

He was making his way through the sky-hued water stealthily lest he disturb the leisure of the swans, drowsy above their own images; lest he discourage the nightingale trying a few low flute notes in the cathedral tower of shadow that was a tree above the tomb of Shakespeare.

The American had never heard a nightingale and it was his first pilgrimage to the shrine of the actor-manager whose productions Americans curiously couple with the Bible as sacred lore.

During the day Joel Wixon had seen the sights of Stratford with the others from his country and from England and the Continent. But now he wanted to get close to Shakespeare. So he hired the skiff and declined the services of the old boat lender.

And now he was stealing up into the rich gloom the church spread across the river. He was pushing the

stern of the boat foremost so that he
eyes. He was making so little speed
sounds were the choked sob of the water
boat cleaved it gently and the tinkle of the dro
fell from the lazy oars with something of the de
music of the uncertain nightingale.

Being a successful business man, Wixon was a su
cated poet. The imagination and the passion and the
orderliness that brought him money were the same
energies that would have made him a success in verse.
But lines were not his line, and he was inarticulate and
incoherent when beauty overwhelmed him, as it did in
nearly every form.

He shivered now before the immediate majesty of
the scene, and the historic meanings that enriched it
as with an embroidered arras. Yet he gave out no
more words than an Eolian harp shuddering with
ecstasy in a wind too gentle to make it audible.

In such moods he hunted solitude, for he was ashamed
to be seen, afraid to be observed in the raptures that
did not belong in the vocabulary of a business man.

He had talked at noon about the fact that he and
Shakespeare's father were in wool, and he had annoyed
a few modest Americans by comparing the petty amount
of the elder Shakespeare's trade with the vast total
pouring from his own innumerable looms driven with
the electricity that the Shakespeares had never dreamed
of.

He had redeemed himself for his pretended brag by
a meek admission:

"But I'm afraid my boy will never write another
'Hamlet.'"

Yet what could he know of his own son? How little
Will Shakespeare's father or his scandalized neighbors

ied that the scapegrace good-for-naught
own for the town's good would make it
nd, coming back to die and lie down for-
ie the Avon, would bring a world of pilgrims
w Mekka, the shrine of the supreme unique poet
human time?

young boy even now was sauntering the path along
the other shore, so lazily tossing pebbles into the stream
that the swans hardly protested. It came upon Wixon
with a kind of silent lightning that Shakespeare had
once been such another boy skipping pebbles across the
narrow river and peering up into the trees to find out
where the nightingale lurked.

Perhaps three hundred years from now some other
shrine would claim the pilgrims, the home perhaps of
some American boy now groping through the amber
mists of adolescence or some man as little revered by
his own neighbors and rivals as the man Shakespeare
was when he went back to Avon to send back to London his two plays a year to the theaters.

Being a practical man, which is a man who strives to
make his visions palpable, Wixon thought of his own
home town and the colony of boys that prospered there
in the Middle West.

He knew that no one would seek the town because
of his birth there, for he was but a buyer of fleeces, a
carder of wools, a spinner of threads, and a weaver of
fabrics to keep folks' bodies warm. His weaves wore
well, but they wore out.

The weavers of words were the ones whose fabrics
lasted beyond the power of time and mocked the moths.
Was there any such spinner in Carthage to give the
town eternal blazon to ears of flesh and blood? There
was one who might have been the man if—

Suddenly he felt himself again in Carthage. There
was a river there too; not a little bolt of chatoyant silk
like the Avon, which they would have called a "crick"
back there. Before Carthage ran the incomprehensible
floods of old Mississippi himself, Father of Waters,
deep and vast and swift. They had lately swung a
weir across it to make it work—a concrete wall a mile
wide and more, and its tumbling cascades spun no little
mill wheels, but swirled thundering turbines that lighted
cities and ran street cars a hundred miles away.

And yet it had no Shakespeare.

And yet again it might have had if—

The twilight was so deep now that he shipped his
oars in the gloom and gave himself back to the past.

He was in another twilight, only it was the counter
twilight between star quench and sun blaze.

Two small boys, himself one of them; his sworn
chum, Luke Mellows, the other, meeting in the silent
street just as the day tide seeped in from the east and
submerged the stars.

Joel had tied a string to his big toe and hung it from
his window. Luke had done the same. They were not
permitted to explode alarm clocks and ruin the last
sweets of sleep in either home. So they had agreed
that the first to wake should rise and dress with stealth,
slip down the dark stairs of his house, into the starlit
street and over to the other's home and pull the toe
cord.

On this morning Luke had been the earlier out, and
his triumphant yanks had dragged Joel feet first from
sleep, and from the bed and almost through the window.
Joel had howled protests in shrill whispers down into
the gloom, and then, untying his outraged toe, had
limped into his clothes and so to the yard.

The two children, in the huge world disputed still by the night, had felt an awe of the sky and the mysteries going on there. The envied man who ran up the streets of evenings lighting the gas street lamps was abroad again already with his little ladder and his quick insect-like motions; only, now he was turning out the lights, just as a similar but invisible being was apparently running around heaven and putting out the stars.

Joel remembered saying: "I wonder if they're turnin' off the stars up there to save gas too."

Luke did not like the joke. He said, using the word "funny" solemnly: "It's funny to see light putting out light. The stars will be there all day, but we won't be able to see 'em for the sun."

(Wixon thought of this now, and of how Shakespeare's fame had drowned out so many stars. A man had told him that there were hundreds of great writers in Shakespeare's time that most people never heard of.)

As the boy paused, the air quivered with a hoarse *moo!* as of a gigantic cow bellowing for her lost calf. It was really a steamboat whistling for the bridge to open the draw and let her through to the south with her raft of logs.

Both of the boys called the boat by name, knowing her voice: "It's the Bessie May Brown!" They started on a run to the bluff overlooking the river, their short legs making a full mile of the scant furlong.

Often as Joel had come out upon the edge of that bluff on his innumerable journeys to the river for fishing, swimming, skating, or just staring, it always smote him with the thrill Balboa must have felt coming suddenly upon the Pacific.

On this morning there was an unwonted grandeur: the whole vault of the sky was curdled with the dawn, a reef of solid black in the west turning to purple and to amber and finally in the east to scarlet, with a few late planets caught in the meshes of the sunlight and trembling like dew on a spider's web.

And the battle in the sky was repeated in the sea-like river with all of the added magic of the current and the eddies and the wimpling rushes of the dawn winds.

On the great slopes were houses and farmsteads throwing off the night and in the river the Bessie May Brown, her red light and her green light trailing scarfs of color on the river, as she chuffed and clanged her bell, and smote the water with her stern wheel. In the little steeple of the pilot house a priest guided her and her unwieldy acre of logs between the piers of the bridge whose lanterns were still belatedly aglow on the girders and again in echo in the flood.

Joel filled his little chest with a gulp of morning air and found no better words for his rhapsody than: "Gee, but ain't it great?"

To his amazement, Luke, who had always been more sensitive than he, shook his head and turned away.

"Gosh, what do you want for ten cents?" Joel demanded, feeling called upon to defend the worthiness of the dawn.

Luke began to cry. He dropped down on his own bare legs in the weeds and twisted his face and his fists in a vain struggle to fight off unmanly grief.

Joel squatted at his side and insisted on sharing the secret; and finally Luke forgot the sense of family honor long enough to yield to the yearning for company in his misery.

"I was up here at midnight last night, and I don't like this place any more."

"You didn't come all by yourself? Gee!"

"No, Momma was here too."

"What she bring you out here at a time like that for?"

"She didn't know I was here."

"Didn't know— What she doin' out here, then?"

"She and Poppa had a turble quar'l. I couldn't hear what started it, but finely it woke me up and I listened, and Momma was cryin' and Poppa was swearin'. And at last Momma said: 'Oh, I might as well go and throw myself in the river,' and Poppa said: 'Good riddance of bad rubbish!' and Momma stopped cryin' and she says: 'All right!' in an awful kind of a voice, and I heard the front door open and shut."

"Gee!"

"Well, I jumped into my shirt and pants and slid down the rain pipe and ran along the street, and there sure enough was Momma walkin' as fast as she could.

"I was afraid to go near her. I don't know why, but I was. So I just sneaked along after her. The street was black as pitch 'cep' for the street lamps, and as she passed ever' one I could see she was still cryin' and stumblin' along like she was blind.

"It was so late we didn't meet anybody at tall, and there wasn't a light in a single house except Joneses, where somebody was sick, I guess. But they didn't pay any attention, and at last she came to the bluff here. And I follered. When she got where she could see the river she stopped and stood there, and held her arms out like she was goin' to jump off or fly, or somethin'. The moon was up, and the river was so bright you could hardly look at it, and Momma stood there with her arms 'way out like she was on the Cross, or something.

"I was so scared and so cold I shook like I had a chill. I was afraid she could hear my teeth chatterin', so I dropped down in the weeds and thistles to keep her from seein' me. It was just along about here too.

"By and by Momma kind of broke like somebody had hit her, then she began to cry again and to walk up and down wringin' her hands. Once or twice she started to run down the bluff and I started to foller; but she stopped like somebody held her back, and I sunk down again.

"Then, after a long time, she shook her head like she couldn't, and turned back. She walked right by me and didn't see me. I heard her whisperin': 'I can't, I can't. My pore children!'

"Then she went back down the street and me after her, wishin' I could go up and help her. But I was afraid she wouldn't want me to know, and I just couldn't go near her."

Luke wept helplessly at the memory of his poltroonery, and Joel tried roughly to comfort him with questions.

"Gee! I don't blame you. I don't guess I could have either. But what was it all about, d'you s'pose?"

"I don't know. Momma went to the front door, and it was locked, and she stood a long, long while before she could bring herself to knock. Then she tapped on it soft like. And by and by Poppa opened the door and said: 'Oh, you're back, are you?' Then he turned and walked away, and she went in.

"I could have killed him with a rock, if she hadn't shut the door. But all I could do was to climb back up the rain pipe. I was so tired and discouraged I nearly fell and broke my neck. And I wisht I had have. But there wasn't any more quar'l, only Momma kind of whimpered once or twice, and Poppa said: 'Oh, for God's sake, shut up and lea' me sleep. I got to open the store in the mornin', ain't I?' I didn't do much sleepin', and I guess that's why I woke up first."

That was all of the story that Joel could learn. The two boys were shut out by the wall of grown-up life. Luke crouched in bitter moodiness, throwing clods of dirt at early grasshoppers and reconquering his lost dignity. At last he said: "If you ever let on to anybody what I told you—"

"Aw, say!" was Joel's protest. His knighthood as a sworn chum was put in question and he was cruelly hurt.

Luke took assurance from his dismay and said in a burst of fury: "Aw, I just said that! I know you won't tell. But just you wait till I can earn a pile of money. I'll take Momma away from that old scoundrel so fast it'll make his head swim!" Then he slumped again. "But it takes so doggone long to grow up, and I don't know how to earn anything."

Then the morning of the world caught into its irresistible vivacity the two boys in the morning of their youth, and before long they had forgotten the irremediable woes of their elders, as their elders also forgot the problems of national woes and cosmic despair.

The boys descended the sidelong path at a jog, brushing the dew and grasshoppers and the birds from the hazel bushes and the papaw shrubs, and scaring many a dewy rabbit from cover.

At the bottom of the bluff the railroad track was the only road along the river, and they began the tormenting passage over the uneven ties with cinders everywhere for their bare feet. They postponed as long as they could the delight of breakfast, and then, sitting on a pile of ties, made a feast of such hard-boiled eggs, cookies, cheese, and crackers as they had been able to wheedle from their kitchens the night before.

Their talk that morning was earnest, as boys' talk is apt to be. They debated their futures as boys are apt to do. Being American boys, two things characterized their plans: one, that the sky itself was the only limit to their ambitions; the other, that they must not follow their fathers' businesses.

Joel's father was an editor; Luke's kept a hardware store.

So Joel wanted to go into trade and Luke wanted to be a writer.

The boys wrangled with the shrill intensity of youth. A stranger passing might have thought them about to come to blows. But they were simply noisy with earnestness. Their argument was as unlike one of the debates in Vergil's Eclogs as possible. It was an antistrophe of twang and drawl:

"Gee, you durned fool, watcha want gointa business for?"

"Durned fool your own self! Watcha wanta be a writer for?"

Then they laughed wildly, struck at each other in mock hostility, and went on with their all-day walk, returning at night too weary for books or even a game of authors or checkers.

Both liked to read, and they were just emerging from the stratum of Old Cap Collier, Nick Carter, the Kid-Glove Miner, and the Steam Man into "Ivanhoe," "Scottish Chiefs," and "Cudjo's Cave." They had passed out of the Oliver Optic, Harry Castlemon, James Otis era.

Joel Wixon read for excitement; Luke Mellows for information as to the machinery of authorship.

Young as they were, they went to the theater—to the op'ra house, which never housed opera.

Joel went often and without price, since his father, being an editor, had the glorious prerogative of "comps." Perhaps that was why Luke wanted to be a writer.

Mr. Mellows, as hard as his own ware, did not believe in the theater and could not be bullied or wept into paying for tickets. But Luke became a program boy and got in free, a precious privilege he kept secret as long as possible, and lost as soon as his father noticed his absences from home on play nights. Then he was whipped for wickedness and ordered to give up the theater forever.

Perhaps Luke would never suffer again so fiercely as he suffered from that denial. It meant a free education and a free revel in the frequent performances of Shakespeare, and of repertory companies that gave such triumphs as "East Lynne" and "Camille," not to mention the road companies that played the uproarious "Peck's Bad Boy," "Over the Garden Wall," "Skipped by the Light of the Moon," and the Charles Hoyt screamers.

The theater had been a cloud-veiled Olympus of mystic exultations, of divine terrors, and of ambrosial laughter. But it was a bad influence. Mr. Mellows's theories of right and wrong were as simple and sharp as his own knives: whatever was delightful and beautiful and laughterful was manifestly wicked, God having plainly devised the pretty things as baits for the devil's fishhooks.

Joel used to tell Luke about the plays he saw, and

the exile's heart ached with envy. They took long
walks up the river or across the bridge into the won-
derlands that were overflowed in high-water times. And
they talked always of their futures. Boyhood was a
torment, a slavery. Heaven was just over the twenty-
first birthday.

Joel got his future, all but the girl he planned to take
with him up the grand stairway of the palace he foresaw. Luke missed his future, and his girl and all of
his dreams.

Between the boys and their manhood stood, as usual,
the fathers, strange monsters, ogres, who seemed to
have forgotten, at the top of the beanstalk, that they
had once been boys themselves down below.

After the early and unceasing misunderstandings as
to motives and standards of honor and dignity came the
civil war over education.

Wouldn't you just know that each boy would get
the wrong dad? Joel's father was proud of Luke and
not of Joel. He had printed some of Luke's poems in
the paper and called him a "precocious" native genius.
Joel's father wished that his boy could have had his
neighbor's boy's gift. It was his sorrow that Joel had
none of the artistic leanings that are called "gifts."
He regretfully gave him up as one who would not carry
on the torch his father had set out with. He could
not force his child to be a genius, but he insisted that
Joel should have an education. The editor had found
himself handicapped by a lack of the mysterious en-
richment that a tour through college gives the least
absorbent mind. He was determined to provide it for
his boy, tho Joel felt that every moment's delay in
leaping into the commercial arena was so much delay
in arriving at gladiatorial eminence.

Luke's father had had even less education than Editor Wixon, but he was proud of it. He had never gone far in the world, but he was one of those men who are automatically proud of everything they do and derive even from failure or humiliation a savage conceit.

He made Luke work in his store or out of it as a delivery boy during vacations from such school terms as the law required. He saw the value of education enough to make out bills and write dunning letters. "Books" to him meant the doleful books that book-keepers keep.

As for any further learning, he thought it a waste of time, a kind of wantonness.

He felt that Providence had intentionally selected a cross for him in the son who was wicked and foolish enough to want to read stories and see plays and go to school for years instead of going right into business.

The thought of sending his boy through a prepara-tory academy and college and wasting his youth on nonsense was outrageous. It maddened him to have the boy plead for such folly. He tried in vain to whip it out of him.

Joel's ideas of education were exactly those of Mr. Mellows, but he did not like Mr. Mellows because of the anguish inflicted on Luke. Joel used to beg Luke to run away from home. But that was impracticable for two reasons: Luke was not of the runaway sort, but meek, and shy, and obedient to a fault.

Besides, while a boy can run away from school, he cannot easily run away to school. If he did, he would be sent back, and if he were not sent back, how was he to pay for his "tooition" and his board and books and clo'es?

It was Luke's influence that sent Joel away to

boardin' school. He so longed to go himself that Joel
felt it foolish to deny himself the godlike opportunity.
So Luke went to school vicariously in Joel, as he got
his other experiences vicariously in books.

At school Joel found so much to do outside of his
classes that he grew content to go all the way. There
was a glee club to manage, also an athletic club; a
paper to solicit ads and subscriptions for; class officers
to be elected, with all the delights of political ma-
neuvering—a world in little to run with all the solemnity
and competition of the adult cosmos. So Joel was
happy and lucky and successful in spite of himself.

The day after Joel took train up the river to his
academy Luke took the position his father secured for
him and entered the little back room where the Butterly
Bottling Works kept its bookkeepers on high stools.

The Butterly soda pop, ginger ales, and other soft
drinks were triumphs of insipidity, and their birch beer
sickened the thirstiest child. But the making and the
marketing and even the drinking of them were matters
of high emprise compared to the keeping of the books.

One of the saddest, sweetest, greatest stories ever
written is Ellis' Pigsispigs Butler's fable of the con-
tented little donkey that went round and round in the
mill and thought he was traveling far. But that donkey
was blind and had no dreams denied.

Luke Mellows was a boy, a boy that still felt his life
in every limb, a boy devoured with fantastic ambitions.
He had a genius within that smothered and struggled
till it all but perished unexpressed. It lived only
enough to be an anguish. It hurt him like a hidden,
unmentioned ingrowing toe nail that cuts and bleeds
and excruciates the fleet member it is meant to protect.

When Joel came home for his first vacation, with the

rush of a young colt that has had a good time in the corral but rejoices in the old pastures, his first cry was for Luke. When he learned where he was, he hurried to the Bottling Works. He was turned away with the curt remark that employees could not be seen in business hours. In those days there were no machines to simplify and verify the bookkeeper's treadmill task, and business hours were never over.

Joel left word at Luke's home for Luke to call for him the minute he was free. He did not come that evening, nor the next. Joel was hurt more than he dared admit.

It was Sunday afternoon before Luke came round, a different Luke, a lean, wan, worn-out shred of a youth. His welcome was sickly.

"Gee-min-*ent*-ly!" Joel roared. "I thought you was mad at me about something. You never came near."

"I wanted to come," Luke croaked, "but nights, I'm too tired to walk anywheres, and besides, I usually have to go back to the offus."

"Gee, that's damn tough," said Joel, who had grown from darn to damn.

Thinking to light Luke up with a congenial theme, Joel heroically forbore to describe the marvels of academy life, and asked: "What you been readin' lately? A little bit of everything, I guess, hey?"

"A whole lot of nothin'," Luke sighed. "I got no strength for readin' by the time I shut my ledgers. I got to save my eyes, you know. The light's bad in that back room."

"What you been writin', then?"

"Miles of figures and entries about one gross bottles lemon, two gross sassaprilla, one gross empties returned."

"No more poetry?"

"No more nothin'."

Joel was obstinately cheerful. "Well, you been makin' money, anyways; that's something."

"Yeh. I buy my own shoes and clo'es now and pay my board and lodgin' at home. And paw puts the two dollars that's left into the savings bank. I got nearly thirty dollars there now. I'll soon have enough for a winter soot and overcoat."

"Gee, can't you go buggy ridin' even with Kit?"

"I could if I had the time and the price, and if her maw wasn't so poorly that Kitty can't get away. I go over there Sunday afternoons sometimes, but her maw always hollers for her to come in. She's afraid to be alone. Kit's had to give up the high school account of her maw."

"How about her goin' away to be a great singer?"

Luke grinned at the insanity of such childish plans. "Oh, that's all off. Kit can't even practice any more. It makes her mother nervous. And Kit had to give up the church choir too. You'd hardly know her. She cries a lot about lookin' so scrawny. O' course I tell her she's pirtier than ever, but that only makes her mad. She can't go to sociables or dances or picnics, and if she could she's got no clo'es. We don't have much fun together; just sit and mope, and then I say: 'Well, guess I better mosey on home,' and she says: 'All right; see you again next Sunday, I s'pose. G'by.'"

The nightingale annoyed the owl and was hushed, and the poet rimed sums in a daybook.

The world waited for them and needed them without knowing it; it would have rewarded them with thrilled attention and wealth and fame. But silence was their portion, silence and the dark and an ache that had no voice.

Joel listened to Luke's elegy and groaned: "Gee!"

But he had an optimism like a powerful spring, and it struck back now with a whir: "I'll tell you what, Luke. Just you wait till I'm rich, then I'll give you a job as vice president, and you can marry Kitty and live on Broadway, in Noo York."

"I've got over believin' in Sandy Claus," said Luke.

Joel saw little of him during this vacation and less during the next. Being by nature a hater of despair, he avoided Luke. He had fits of remorse for this, and once he dared to make a personal appeal to old Mr. Mellows to send Luke away to school. He was received with scant courtesy, and only tolerated because he gave the father a chance to void some of his bile at the worthlessness of Luke.

"He's no good; that's what's the matter of him. And wilful too—he just mopes around because he wants to show me I'm wrong. But he's only cuttin' off his own nose to spite his face. I'll learn him who's got the most will power."

Joel was bold enough to suggest: "Maybe Luke would be differ'nt if you'd let him go to college. You know, Mr. Mellows, if you'll 'scuse my saying it, there's some natures that are differ'nt from others. You hitch a race horse up to a plow and you spoil a good horse and your field both. Seems to me as if, if Luke got a chance to be a writer or a professor or something, he might turn out to be a wonder. You can't teach a canary bird to be a hen, you know, and—"

Mr. Mellows locked himself in that ridiculous citadel of ancient folly. "When you're as old as I am, Joel, you'll know more. The first thing anybody's got to learn in this world is to respect their parents."

Joel wanted to say: "I should think that depended on the parents."

But, of course, he kept silent, as the young usually do when they hear the old maundering, and he gave up as he heard the stupid dolt returning to his old refrain: "I left school when I was twelve years old. Ain't had a day since, and I can't say as I've been exactly a failure. Best hardware store in Carthage and holdin' my own in spite of bad business."

Joel slunk away, unconvinced but baffled. One summer he brought all his pressure to bear on Luke to persuade him to run away from his job and strike out for the big city where the big opportunities grew.

But Luke shook his head. He lacked initiative. Perhaps that was where his talent was not genius. It blistered him, but it made no steam.

Shakespeare had known enough to leave Stratford. He had had to hold horses outside the theater, and even then he had organized a little business group of horse holders called "Shakespeare's boys." He had the business sense, and he forced his way into the theater and became a stockholder. Shakespeare was always an adventurer. He had to work in a butcher's shop, but before he was nineteen he was already married to a woman of twenty-six, and none too soon for the first child's sake.

Luke Mellows had not the courage or the recklessness to marry Kitty, tho he had as good a job as Shakespeare's. Shakespeare would not let a premature family keep him from his ambition.

He was twenty-one when he went to London, but he went.

London was a boom town then, about the size of Trenton, or Grand Rapids, or Spokane, and growing fast. Boys were running away from the farms and villages as they always have done. Other boys went to London from Stratford. John Sadler became a big wholesale grocer, and Richard Field a publisher. They had as various reasons then as now.

But the main thing was that they left home. That might mean a noble or a selfish ambition, but it took action.

Luke Mellows would not go. He dreaded to abandon his mother to the father who bullied them both. He could not bear to leave Kitty alone with the wretched mother who ruled her with tears.

Other boys ran or walked away from Carthage, some of them to become failures, and some half successes, and some of them to acquire riches and power. And other boys stayed at home.

Girls, too, had won obscurity by inertia or had swung into fame. Some of the girls had stayed at home and gone wrong there. Some had gone away in disgrace, and redeemed or damned themselves in larger parishes. There were Aspasias and Joans of Arc in miniature, minor Florence Nightingales and Melbas and Rosa Bonheurs. But they had all had to leap from the nest and try their wings. Of those that did not take the plunge, none made the flight.

Cowardice held some back, but the purest self-sacrifice others. Joel felt that there ought to be a heaven for these latter, yet he hoped that there was no hell for the former. For who can save himself from his own timidity, and who can protect himself from his own courage?

Given that little spur of initiative, that little armor

of selfish indifference to the clinging hands at home, and how many a soul might not have reached the stars? Look at the women who were crowding the rolls of fame of late just because all womankind had broken free of the apron strings of alleged respectability.

Joel had no proof that Luke Mellows would have amounted to much. Perhaps, if he had ventured over the nest's edge, he would have perished on the ground, trampled into dust by the fameward mob, or devoured by the critics that pounce upon every fledgling and suck the heart out of all that cannot fling them off.

But Joel could not surrender his childhood faith that Luke Mellows had been meant for another Shakespeare. Yet Mellows had never written a play or an act of a play. But, for that matter, neither had Shakespeare before he went to London. He was only a poet at first, and some of his poems were pretty poor stuff—if you took Shakespeare's name off it. And his first poems had to be published by his fellow townsman Field.

There were the childish poems by Luke Mellows that Joel's father had published in the Carthage "Clarion." Joel had forgotten them utterly, and they were probably meritorious of oblivion. But there was one poem Luke had written that Joel memorized.

It appeared in the "Clarion" years after Joel was a success in wool. His father still sent him the paper, and in one number Joel was rejoiced to read these lines:

THE ANONYMOUS
By LUKE MELLOWS

Sometimes at night within a wooded park
  Like an ocean cavern, fathoms deep in bloom,
  Sweet scents, like hymns, from hidden flowers fume,
And make the wanderer happy, tho the dark
  Obscures their tint, their name, their shapely bloom.

So, in the thick-set chronicles of fame,
  There hover deathless feats of souls unknown.
  They linger like the fragrant smoke wreaths blown
From liberal sacrifice. Gone face and name;
  The deeds, like homeless ghosts, live on alone.

Wixon, seated in the boat on Avon and lost in such
dusk that he could hardly see his hand upon the idle
oar, recited the poem softly to himself, intoning it in
the deep voice one saves for poetry. It sounded wonderful to him in the luxury of hearing his own voice
upon the water and indulging his own memory. The
somber mood was perfect, in accord with the realm of
shadow and silence where everything beautiful and
living was cloaked in the general blur.

After he had heard his voice chanting the last long
oh's of the final verse, he was ashamed of his solemnity,
and terrified lest some one might have heard him and
accounted him insane. He laughed at himself for a
sentimental fool.

He laughed too as he remembered what a letter of
praise he had dictated to his astonished stenographer
and fired off at Luke Mellows; and at the flippant
letter he had in return.

Lay leaders who send incandescent epistles to poets
are apt to receive answers in sardonic prose. The poet
lies a little, perhaps, in a very sane suspicion of his
own transcendencies.

Luke Mellows had written:

"DEAR OLD JOEL:
  "I sure am much obliged for your mighty handsome
letter. Coming to one of the least successful wool-
gatherers in the world from one of the most successful
wool distributors, it deserves to be highly prized. And
is. I will have it framed and handed down to my heirs,

of which there are more than there will ever be looms.

"You ask me to tell you all about myself. It won't take long. When the Butterly Bottlery went bust, I had no job at all for six months, so I got married to spite my father. And to please Kit, whose poor mother ceased to suffer about the same time.

"The poor girl was so used to taking care of a poor old woman who couldn't be left alone that I became her patient just to keep all her talents from going to waste.

"The steady flow of children seems to upset the law of supply and demand, for there is certainly no demand for more of my progeny and there is no supply for them. But somehow they thrive.

"I am now running my father's store, as the old gentleman had a stroke and then another. The business is going to pot as rapidly as you would expect, but I haven't been able to kill it off quite yet.

"Thanks for advising me to go on writing immortal poetry. If I were immortal, I might, but that fool thing was the result of about ten years' hard labor. I tried to make a sonnet of it, but I gave up at the end of the decade and called it whatever it is.

"Your father's paper published it free of charge, and so my income from my poetry has been one-tenth of nothing per annum. Please don't urge me to do any more. I really can't afford it.

"The poem was suggested to me by an ancient fit of blues over the fact that Kit's once-so-beautiful voice would never be heard in song, and by the fact that her infinite goodnesses will never meet any recompense or even acknowledgment.

"I was bitter the first five years, but the last five years I began to feel how rich this dark old world is in good, brave, sweet, lovable, heartbreakingly beautiful deeds that simply cast a little fragrance on the dark and are gone. They perfume the night and the busy daylight dispels them like the morning mists that we used to watch steaming and vanishing above the old river. The Mississippi is still here, still rolling along its eternal multitudes of snows and flowers and fruits and fish and snakes and dead men and boats and trees.

"They go where they came from, I guess—in and out of nothing and back again.

"It is a matter of glory to all of us that you are doing so nobly. Keep it up and give us something to brag about in our obscurity. Don't worry. We are happy enough in the dark. We have our batlike sports and our owllike prides, and the full sun would blind us and lose us our way.

"Kit sends you her love—and blushes as she says it. That is a very daring word for such shy moles as we are, but I will echo it.

"Yours for old sake's sake.   LUKE."

Vaguely remembering this letter now Joel inhaled a bit of the merciful chloroform that deadens the pain of thwarted ambition.

The world was full of men and women like Luke and Kit. Some had given up great hopes because they were too good to tread others down in their quest. Some had quenched great talents because they were too fearsome or too weak or too lazy to feed their lamps with oil and keep them trimmed and alight. Some had stumbled through life darkly with no gifts of talent, without even appreciation of the talents of others or of the flowerlike beauties that star the meadows.

Those were the people he had known. And then there were the people he had not known, the innumerable caravan that had passed across the earth while he lived, the inconceivable hosts that had gone before, tribe after tribe, generation upon generation, nation at the heels of nation, cycle on era on age, and the backward perpetuity from everlasting unto everlasting. People, people, people—poor souls, until the thronged stars that make a dust of the Milky Way were a lesser mob.

Here in this graveyard at Stratford lay men who might have overtopped Shakespeare's glory if they had but "had a mind to." Some of them had been held in higher esteem in their town. But they were forgotten, their names leveled with the surface of their fallen tombstones.

Had he not cried out in his own Hamlet: "O God, I could be bounded in a nutshell and count myself a king of infinite space, were it not that I have bad dreams—which dreams indeed are ambition; for the very substance of the ambitious is merely the shadow of a dream—and I hold ambition of so airy and light a quality that it is but a shadow's shadow."

After all, the greatest of men were granted but a lesser oblivion than the least. And in that overpowering thought there was a strange comfort, the comfort of misery finding itself in an infinite company.

The night was thick upon Avon. The swans had gone somewhere. The lights in the houses had a sleepy look. It was time to go to bed.

Joel yawned with the luxury of having wearied his heart with emotion. He had thought himself out for once. It was good to be tired. He put his oars into the stream and, dipping up reflected stars, sent them swirling in a doomsday chaos after him with the defiant revenge of a proud soul who scorns the universe that grinds him to dust.

The old boatman was surly with waiting. He did not thank the foreigner for his liberal largeness, and did not answer his good night.

As Wixon left the river and took the road for his hotel, the nightingale (that forever anonymous nightingale, only one among the millions of forgotten or throttled songsters) revolted for a moment or two against the stifling doom and shattered it with a wordless sonnet of fierce and beautiful protest—"The tawny-throated! What triumph! hark!—what pain!"

It was as if Luke Mellows had suddenly found expression in something better than words, something that any ear could understand, an ache that rang.

Wixon stopped, transfixed as by flaming arrows. He could not understand what the bird meant or what he meant, nor could the bird. But as there is no laughter that eases the heart like unpacking it of its woes in something beyond wording, so there is nothing that brightens the eyes like tears gushing without shame or restraint.

Joel Wixon felt that it was a good, sad, mad world, and that he had been very close to Shakespeare—so close that he heard things nobody had ever found the phrases for—things that cannot be said but only felt, and transmitted rather by experience than by expression from one proud worm in the mud to another.

THE LONG EXILE

By Count Leo Tolstoy

(Leo Tolstoy, 1828-1910.)

Tolstoy is the most celebrated of all Russian writers. This extrordinary man, after serving in the army as a young man and leading a wild and reckless life, was for half a century the great interpreter of the life of his country, and during the last thirty years a religious and social prophet. He was preeminent as a novelist, tho his complete works include a large number of fairy tales and short stories.

The present version has been reprinted from Thomas Seltzer's *Best Russian Short Stories*, Boni & Liveright, New York, by whose permission it is here used.

In the town of Vladimir lived a young merchant named Ivan Dmitrich Aksionov. He had two shops and a house of his own.

Aksionov was a handsome, fair-haired, curly-headed fellow, full of fun, and very fond of singing. When quite a young man he had been given to drink, and was riotous when he had had too much; but after he married he gave up drinking, except now and then.

One summer Aksionov was going to the Nizhny

Fair, and as he bade good-bye to his family, his wife said to him, "Ivan Dmitrich, do not start to-day; I have had a bad dream about you."

Aksionov laughed, and said, "You are afraid that when I get to the fair I shall go on a spree."

His wife replied: "I do not know what I am afraid of; all I know is that I had a bad dream. I dreamt you returned from the town, and when you took off your cap I saw that your hair was quite gray."

Aksionov laughed. "That's a lucky sign," said he. "See if I don't sell out all my goods, and bring you some presents from the fair."

So he said good-bye to his family, and drove away.

When he had traveled half-way, he met a merchant whom he knew, and they put up at the same inn for the night. They had some tea together, and then went to bed in adjoining rooms.

It was not Aksionov's habit to sleep late, and wishing to travel while it was still cool, he aroused his driver before dawn, and told him to put in the horses.

Then he made his way across to the landlord of the inn (who lived in a cottage at the back), paid his bill, and continued his journey.

When he had gone about twenty-five miles, he stopped for the horses to be fed. Aksionov rested awhile in the passage of the inn, then he stepped out into the porch, and, ordering a samovar to be heated, got out his guitar and began to play.

Suddenly a troika drove up with tinkling bells and an official alighted, followed by two soldiers. He came to Aksionov and began to question him, asking him who he was and whence he came. Aksionov answered him fully, and said, "Won't you have some tea with me?" But the official went on cross-questioning him and asking him, "Where did you spend last night? Were you alone, or with a fellow-merchant? Did you see the other merchant this morning? Why did you leave the inn before dawn?"

Aksionov wondered why he was asked all these questions, but he described all that had happened, and then added, "Why do you cross-question me as if I were a thief or a robber? I am traveling on business of my own, and there is no need to question me."

Then the official, calling the soldiers, said, "I am the police-officer of this district, and I question you because the merchant with whom you spent last night has been found with his throat cut. We must search your things."

They entered the house. The soldiers and the police-officer unstrapped Aksionov's luggage and searched it. Suddenly the officer drew a knife out of a bag, crying, "Whose knife is this?"

Aksionov looked, and seeing a blood-stained knife taken from his bag, he was frightened.

"How is it there is blood on this knife?"

Aksionov tried to answer, but could hardly utter a word, and only stammered: "I—don't know—not mine."

Then the police-officer said: "This morning the merchant was found in bed with his throat cut. You are the only person who could have done it. The house was locked from inside, and no one else was there. Here is this blood-stained knife in your bag, and your face and manner betray you! Tell me how you killed him, and how much money you stole?"

Aksionov swore he had not done it; that he had not seen the merchant after they had had tea together; that he had no money except eight thousand rubles of his own, and that the knife was not his. But his voice was broken, his face pale, and he trembled with fear as tho he were guilty.

The police-officer ordered the soldiers to bind Aksionov and to put him in the cart. As they tied his feet together and flung him into the cart, Aksionov crossed himself and wept. His money and goods were taken from him, and he was sent to the nearest town and imprisoned there. Inquiries as to his character were made in Vladimir. The merchants and other inhabitants of that town said that in former days he used to drink and waste his time, but that he was a good man. Then the trial came on: he was charged with murdering a merchant from Ryazan, and robbing him of twenty thousand rubles.

His wife was in despair, and did not know what to believe. Her children were all quite small; one was a baby at her breast. Taking them all with her, she went to the town where her husband was in jail. At first she was not allowed to see him; but after much begging, she obtained permission from the officials, and was taken to him. When she saw her husband in prison-dress and in chains, shut up with thieves and criminals, she fell down, and did not come to her senses for a long time. Then she drew her children to her, and sat down near him. She told him of things at home, and asked about what had happened to him. He told her all, and she asked, "What can we do now?"

"We must petition the Czar not to let an innocent man perish."

His wife told him that she had sent a petition to the Czar, but it had not been accepted.

Aksionov did not reply, but only looked downcast.

Then his wife said, "It was not for nothing I

dreamt your hair had turned gray. You remember? You should not have started that day." And passing her fingers through his hair, she said: "Vanya dearest, tell your wife the truth; was it not you who did it?"

"So you, too, suspect me!" said Aksionov, and, hiding his face in his hands, he began to weep. Then a soldier came to say that the wife and children must go away; and Aksionov said good-by to his family for the last time.

When they were gone, Aksionov recalled what had been said, and when he remembered that his wife also had suspected him, he said to himself, "It seems that only God can know the truth; it is to Him alone we must appeal, and from Him alone expect mercy."

And Aksionov wrote no more petitions; gave up all hope, and only prayed to God.

Aksionov was condemned to be flogged and sent to the mines. So he was flogged with a knout, and when the wounds made by the knout were healed, he was driven to Siberia with other convicts.

For twenty-six years Aksionov lived as a convict in Siberia. His hair turned white as snow, and his beard grew long, thin, and gray. All his mirth went; he stooped; he walked slowly, spoke little, and never laughed, but he often prayed.

In prison Aksionov learned to make boots, and earned a little money, with which he bought *The Lives of the Saints*. He read this book when there was light enough in the prison; and on Sundays in the prison-church he read the lessons and sang in the choir; for his voice was still good.

The prison authorities liked Aksionov for his meekness, and his fellow-prisoners respected him: they called him "Grandfather," and "The Saint." When they wanted to petition the prison authorities about anything, they always made Aksionov their spokesman, and when there were quarrels among the prisoners they came to him to put things right, and to judge the matter.

No news reached Aksionov from his home, and he did not even know if his wife and children were still alive.

One day a fresh gang of convicts came to the prison. In the evening the old prisoners collected round the new ones and asked them what towns or villages they came from, and what they were sentenced for. Among the rest Aksionov sat down near the newcomers, and listened with downcast air to what was said.

One of the new convicts, a tall, strong man of sixty, with a closely-cropped gray beard, was telling the others what he had been arrested for.

"Well, friends," he said, "I only took a horse that was tied to a sledge, and I was arrested and accused of stealing. I said I had only taken it to get home quicker, and had then let it go; besides, the driver was a personal friend of mine. So I said, 'It's all right.' 'No,' said they, 'you stole it.' But how or where I stole it they could not say. I once really did something wrong, and ought by rights to have come here long ago, but that time I was not found out. Now I have been sent here for nothing at all. . . . Eh, but it's lies I'm telling you; I've been to Siberia before, but I did not stay long."

"Where are you from?" asked some one.

"From Vladimir. My family are of that town. My name is Makar, and they also call me Semyonich."

Aksionov raised his head and said: "Tell me, Semyonich, do you know anything of the merchants Aksionov of Vladimir? Are they still alive?"

"Know them? Of course I do. The Aksionovs are rich, tho their father is in Siberia: a sinner like ourselves, it seems! As for you, Gran'dad, how did you come here?"

Aksionov did not like to speak of his misfortune. He only sighed, and said, "For my sins I have been in prison these twenty-six years."

"What sins?" asked Makar Semyonich.

But Aksionov only said, "Well, well—I must have deserved it!" He would have said no more, but his companions told the newcomers how Aksionov came to be in Siberia; how some one had killed a merchant, and had put the knife among Aksionov's things, and Aksionov had been unjustly condemned.

When Makar Semyonich heard this, he looked at Aksionov, slapped his own knee, and exclaimed, "Well, this is wonderful! Really wonderful! But how old you've grown, Gran'dad!"

The others asked him why he was so surprised, and where he had seen Aksionov before; but Makar Semyonich did not reply. He only said: "It's wonderful that we should meet here, lads!"

These words made Aksionov wonder whether this man knew who had killed the merchant; so he said, "Perhaps, Semyonich, you have heard of that affair, or maybe you've seen me before?"

"How could I help hearing? The world's full of rumors. But it's a long time ago, and I've forgotten what I heard."

"Perhaps you heard who killed the merchant?" asked Aksionov.

Makar Semyonich laughed, and replied: "It must

have been him in whose bag the knife was found! If some one else hid the knife there, 'He's not a thief till he's caught,' as the saying is. How could any one put a knife into your bag while it was under your head? It would surely have woke you up."

When Aksionov heard these words, he felt sure this was the man who had killed the merchant. He rose and went away. All that night Aksionov lay awake. He felt terribly unhappy, and all sorts of images rose in his mind. There was the image of his wife as she was when he parted from her to go to the fair. He saw her as if she were present; her face and her eyes rose before him; he heard her speak and laugh. Then he saw his children, quite little, as they were at that time: one with a little cloak on, another at his mother's breast. And then he remembered himself as he used to be—young and merry. He remembered how he sat playing the guitar in the porch of the inn where he was arrested, and how free from care he had been. He saw, in his mind, the place where he was flogged, the executioner, and the people standing around; the chains, the convicts, all the twenty-six years of his prison life, and his premature old age. The thought of it all made him so wretched that he was ready to kill himself.

"And it's all that villain's doing!" thought Aksionov. And his anger was so great against Makar Semyonich that he longed for vengeance, even if he himself should perish for it. He kept repeating prayers all night, but could get no peace. During the day he did not go near Makar Semyonich, nor even look at him.

A fortnight passed in this way. Aksionov could not sleep at night, and was so miserable that he did not know what to do.

One night as he was walking about the prison he noticed some earth that came rolling out from under one of the shelves on which the prisoners slept. He stopped to see what it was. Suddenly Makar Semyonich crept out from under the shelf, and looked up at Aksionov with frightened face. Aksionov tried to pass without looking at him, but Makar seized his hand and told him that he had dug a hole under the wall, getting rid of the earth by putting it into his high-boots, and emptying it out every day on the road when the prisoners were driven to their work.

"Just you keep quiet, old man, and you shall get out too. If you blab, they'll flog the life out of me, but I will kill you first."

Aksionov trembled with anger as he looked at his enemy. He drew his hand away, saying, "I have no wish to escape, and you have no need to kill me; you killed me long ago! As to telling of you—I may do so or not as God shall direct."

Next day, when the convicts were led out to work, the convoy soldiers noticed that one or other of the prisoners emptied some earth out of his boots. The prison was searched and the tunnel found. The Governor came and questioned all the prisoners to find out who had dug the hole. They all denied any knowledge of it. Those who knew would not betray Makar Semyonich, knowing he would be flogged almost to death. At last the Governor turned to Aksionov whom he knew to be a just man, and said:

"You are a truthful old man; tell me, before God, who dug the hole?"

Makar Semyonich stood as if he were quite unconcerned, looking at the Governor and not so much as glancing at Aksionov. Aksionov's lips and hands trembled, and for a long time he could not utter a word. He thought, "Why should I screen him who ruined my life? Let him pay for what I have suffered. But if I tell, they will probably flog the life out of him, and maybe I suspect him wrongly. And, after all, what good would it be to me?"

"Well, old man," repeated the Governor, "tell me the truth: who has been digging under the wall?"

Aksionov glanced at Makar Semyonich, and said, "I cannot say, your honor. It is not God's will that I should tell! Do what you like with me; I am in your hands."

However much the Governor tried, Aksionov would say no more, and so the matter had to be left.

That night, when Aksionov was lying on his bed and just beginning to doze, some one came quietly and sat down on his bed. He peered through the darkness and recognized Makar.

"What more do you want of me?" asked Aksionov. "Why have you come here?"

Makar Semyonich was silent. So Aksionov sat up and said, "What do you want? Go away, or I will call the guard!"

Makar Semyonich bent close over Aksionov, and whispered, "Ivan Dmitrich, forgive me!"

"What for?" asked Aksionov.

"It was I who killed the merchant and hid the knife among your things. I meant to kill you too, but I heard a noise outside, so I hid the knife in your bag and escaped out of the window."

Aksionov was silent, and did not know what to say. Makar Semyonich slid off the bed-shelf and knelt upon the ground. "Ivan Dmitrich," said he, "forgive me! For the love of God, forgive me! I will confess that it was I who killed the merchant, and you will be released and can go to your home."

"It is easy for you to talk," said Aksionov, "but I have suffered for you these twenty-six years. Where could I go to now? . . . My wife is dead, and my children have forgotten me. I have nowhere to go. . . ."

Makar Semyonich did not rise, but beat his head on the floor. "Ivan Dmitrich, forgive me!" he cried. "When they flogged me with the knout it was not so hard to bear as it is to see you now . . . yet you had pity on me, and did not tell. For Christ's sake, forgive me, wretch that I am!" And he began to sob.

When Aksionov heard him sobbing he, too, began to weep.

"God will forgive you!" said he. "Maybe I am a hundred times worse than you." And at these words his heart grew light, and the longing for home left him. He no longer had any desire to leave the prison, but only hoped for his last hour to come.

In spite of what Aksionov had said, Makar Semyonich confessed his guilt. But when the order for his release came, Aksionov was already dead.

THE PROPHETIC PICTURES[1]

By Nathaniel Hawthorne

"But this painter!" cried Walter Ludlow, with animation. "He not only excels in his peculiar art, but possesses vast acquirements in all other learning and science. He talks Hebrew with Dr. Mather, and gives lectures in anatomy to Dr. Boylston. In a word, he will meet the best instructed man among us, on his own ground. Moreover, he is a polished gentleman—a citizen of the world—yes, a true cosmopolite; for he will speak like a native of each clime and country on the globe, except our own forests, whither he is now going. Nor is all this what I most admire in him."

"Indeed!" said Elinor, who had listened with a woman's interest to the description of such a man. "Yet this is admirable enough."

"Surely it is," replied her lover, "but far less so than his natural gift of adapting himself to every variety of character, insomuch that all men—and all women too, Elinor—shall find a mirror of themselves in this wonderful painter. But the greatest wonder is yet to be told."

"Nay, if he have more wonderful attributes than these," said Elinor, laughing, "Boston is a perilous

[1] This story was suggested by an anecdote of Stuart, related in Dunlap's "History of the Arts of Design"—a most entertaining book to the general reader, and a deeply interesting one, we should think, to the artist.

abode for the poor gentleman. Are you telling me of a painter, or a wizard?"

"In truth," answered he, "that question might be asked much more seriously than you suppose. They say that he paints not merely a man's features, but his mind and heart. He catches the secret sentiments and passions, and throws them upon the canvas, like sunshine—or perhaps, in the portraits of dark-souled men, like a gleam of infernal fire. It is an awful gift," added Walter, lowering his voice from its tone of enthusiasm. "I shall be almost afraid to sit to him."

"Walter, are you in earnest?" exclaimed Elinor.

"For Heaven's sake, dearest Elinor, do not let him paint the look which you now wear," said her lover smiling, tho rather perplexed. "There: it is passing away now but when you spoke you seemed frightened to death, and very sad besides. What were you thinking of?"

"Nothing, nothing," answered Elinor, hastily. "You paint my face with your own fantasies. Well, come for me tomorrow, and we will visit this wonderful artist."

But when the young man had departed, it cannot be denied that a remarkable expression was again visible on the fair and youthful face of his mistress. It was a sad and anxious look, little in accordance with what should have been the feelings of a maiden on the eve of wedlock. Yet Walter Ludlow was the chosen of her heart.

"A look!" said Elinor to herself. "No wonder that it startled him, if it expressed what I sometimes feel. I know, by my own experience, how frightful a look may be. But it was all fancy. I thought nothing

of it at the time—I have seen nothing of it since—
I did but dream it."

And she busied herself about the embroidery of a
ruff, in which she meant that her portrait should be
taken.

The painter of whom they had been speaking was
not one of those native artists who, at a later period
than this, borrowed their colors from the Indians, and
manufactured their pencils of the furs of wild beasts.
Perhaps, if he could have revoked his life and pre-
arranged his destiny, he might have chosen to belong
to that school without a master, in the hope of being
at least original, since there were no works of art to
imitate, nor rules to follow. But he had been born
and educated in Europe. People said that he had
studied the grandeur or beauty of conception, and every
touch of the master-hand, in all the most famous pictures, in cabinets and galleries, and on the walls of
churches, till there was nothing more for his powerful
mind to learn. Art could add nothing to its lessons,
but Nature might. He had therefore visited a world
whither none of his professional brethren had preceded
him, to feast his eyes on visible images that were noble
and picturesque, yet had never been transferred to
canvas. America was too poor to afford other tempta-
tions to an artist of eminence, tho many of the
colonial gentry, on the painter's arrival, had expressed
a wish to transmit their lineaments to posterity by
means of his skill. Whenever such proposals were
made, he fixed his piercing eyes on the applicant, and
seemed to look him through and through. If he
beheld only a sleek and comfortable visage, tho
there were a gold-laced coat to adorn the picture, and
golden guineas to pay for it, he civilly rejected the task

and the reward. But if the face were the index of
anything uncommon, in thought, sentiment, or experience; or if he met a beggar in the street, with a white
beard and a furrowed brow; or if sometimes a child
happened to look up and smile; he would exhaust all
the art on them that he denied to wealth.

Pictorial skill being so rare in the colonies, the
painter became an object of general curiosity. If few
or none could appreciate the technical merit of his
productions, yet there were points in regard to which
the opinion of the crowd was as valuable as the refined
judgment of the amateur. He watched the effect that
each picture produced on such untutored beholders, and
derived profit from their remarks, while they would as
soon have thought of instructing Nature herself as
him who seemed to rival her. Their admiration, it
must be owned, was tinctured with the prejudices of
the age and country. Some deemed it an offense
against the Mosaic law, and even a presumptuous
mockery of the Creator, to bring into existence such
lively images of His creatures. Others, frightened at
the art which could raise fantoms at will, and keep
the form of the dead among the living, were inclined
to consider the painter as a magician, or perhaps the
famous Black Man, of old witch-times, plotting mis-
chief in a new guise. These foolish fancies were more
than half believed among the mob. Even in superior
circles, his character was invested with a vague awe,
partly rising like smoke-wreaths from the popular
superstitions, but chiefly caused by the varied knowledge and talents which he made subservient to his
profession.

Being on the eve of marriage, Walter Ludlow and
Elinor were eager to obtain their portraits, as the first

of what, they doubtless hoped, would be a long series of family pictures. The day after the conversation above recorded, they visited the painter's rooms. A servant ushered them into an apartment, where, tho the artist himself was not visible, there were personages whom they could hardly forbear greeting with reverence. They knew, indeed, that the whole assembly were but pictures, yet felt it impossible to separate the idea of life and intellect from such striking counterfeits. Several of the portraits were known to them, either as distinguished characters of the day, or their private acquaintances. There was Governor Burnet, looking as if he had just received an undutiful communication from the House of Representatives, and were inditing a most sharp response. Mr. Cooke hung beside the ruler whom he opposed, sturdy, and somewhat puritanical, as befitted a popular leader. The ancient lady of Sir William Phips eyed them from the wall, in ruff and farthingale, an imperious old dame, not unsuspected of witchcraft. John Winslow, then a very young man, wore the expression of warlike enterprise which long afterward made him a distinguished general. Their personal friends were recognized at a glance. In most of the pictures, the whole mind and character were brought out on the countenance, and concentrated into a single look, so that, to speak paradoxically, the originals hardly resembled themselves so strikingly as the portraits did.

Among these modern worthies, there were two old bearded saints, who had almost vanished into the darkening canvas. There was also a pale but unfaded Madonna, who had perhaps been worshiped in Rome, and now regarded the lovers with such a mild and holy look that they longed to worship too.

"How singular a thought," observed Walter Ludlow, "that this beautiful face has been beautiful for above two hundred years! Oh, if all beauty would endure so well! Do you not envy her, Elinor?"

"If earth were heaven, I might," she replied. "But where all things fade, how miserable to be one that could not fade!"

"This dark old St. Peter has a fierce and ugly scowl, saint tho he be," continued Walter. "He troubles me. But the virgin looks kindly at us."

"Yes; but very sorrowfully, methinks," said Elinor. The easel stood beneath these three old pictures, sustaining one that had been recently commenced. After a little inspection, they began to recognize the features of their own minister, the Rev. Dr. Colman, growing into shape and life as it were, out of a cloud.

"Kind old man!" exclaimed Elinor. "He gazes at me as if he were about to utter a word of paternal advice."

"And at me," said Walter, "as if he were about to shake his head and rebuke me for some suspected iniquity. But so does the original. I shall never feel quite comfortable under his eye, till we stand before him to be married."

They now heard a footstep on the floor, and turning, beheld the painter, who had been some moments in the room, and had listened to a few of their remarks. He was a middle-aged man, with a countenance well worthy of his own pencil. Indeed, by the picturesque tho careless arrangement of his rich dress, and, perhaps, because his soul dwelt always among painted shapes, he looked somewhat like a portrait himself. His visitors were sensible of a kindred between the artist and his works, and felt as if one of the pictures had stepped from the canvas to salute them.

Walter Ludlow, who was slightly known to the painter, explained the object of their visit. While he spoke, a sunbeam was falling athwart his figure and Elinor's, with so happy an effect that they also seemed living pictures of youth and beauty, gladdened by bright fortune. The artist was evidently struck.

"My easel is occupied for several ensuing days, and my stay in Boston must be brief," said he, thoughtfully; then, after an observant glance, he added, "but your wishes shall be gratified, tho I disappoint the Chief-Justice and Madam Oliver. I must not lose this opportunity, for the sake of painting a few wells of broadcloth and brocade."

The painter expressed a desire to introduce both their portraits into one picture, and represent them engaged in some appropriate action. This plan would have delighted the lovers, but was necessarily rejected, because so large a space of canvas would have been unfit for the room which it was intended to decorate. Two half-length portraits were therefore fixed upon. After they had taken leave, Walter Ludlow asked Elinor, with a smile, whether she knew what an influence over their fates the painter was about to acquire.

"The old women of Boston affirm," continued he, "that after he has once got possession of a person's face and figures, he may paint him in any act or situation whatever—and the picture will be prophetic. Do you believe it?"

"Not quite," said Elinor, smiling. "Yet if he has such magic, there is something so gentle in his manner that I am sure he will use it well."

It was the painter's choice to proceed with both the portraits at the same time, assigning as a reason, in the mystical language which he sometimes used, that the faces threw light upon each other. Accordingly, he gave now a touch to Walter, and now to Elinor, and the features of one and the other began to start forth so vividly that it appeared as if his triumphant art would actually disengage them from the canvas. Amid the rich light and deep shade they beheld their fantom selves. But tho the likeness promised to be perfect they were not quite satisfied with the expression; it seemed more vague than in most of the painter's works. He, however, was satisfied with the prospect of success, and being much interested in the lovers, employed his leisure moments, unknown to them, in making a crayon sketch of their two figures. During their sittings, he engaged them in conversation, and kindled up their faces with characteristic traits, which, tho continually varying, it was his purpose to combine and fix. At length he announced that at their next visit both the portraits would be ready for delivery.

"If my pencil will but be true to my conception, in the few last touches which I meditate," observed he, "these two pictures will be my very best performances. Seldom, indeed, has an artist such subjects."

While speaking, he still bent his penetrative eye upon them, nor withdrew it till they had reached the bottom of the stairs.

Nothing, in the whole circle of human vanities, takes stronger hold of the imagination than this affair of having a portrait painted. Yet why should it be so? The looking-glass, the polished globes of the andirons, the mirror-like water, and all other reflecting surfaces, continually present us with portraits, or rather ghosts, of ourselves, which we glance at, and straightway forget them. But we forget them only because they vanish. It is the idea of duration—of earthly immortality—that gives such a mysterious interest to our own portraits. Walter and Elinor were not insensible to this feeling, and hastened to the painter's room, punctually at the appointed hour, to meet those pictured shapes which were to be their representatives with posterity. The sunshine flashed after them into the apartment, but left it somewhat gloomy, as they closed the door.

Their eyes were immediately attracted to their portraits, which rested against the furthest wall of the room. At the first glance, through the dim light and the distance, seeing themselves in precisely their natural attitudes, and with all the air that they recognized so well, they uttered a simultaneous exclamation of delight.

"There we stand," cried Walter, enthusiastically, "fixed in sunshine forever! No dark passions can gather on our faces!"

"No," said Elinor, more calmly; "no dreary change can sadden us."

This was said while they were approaching, and had yet gained only an imperfect view of the pictures. The painter, after saluting them, busied himself at a table in completing a crayon sketch, leaving his visitors to form their own judgment as to his perfected labors. At intervals, he sent a glance from beneath his deep eyebrows, watching their countenances in profile, with his pencil suspended over the sketch. They had now stood some moments, each in front of the other's picture, contemplating it with entranced attention, but without uttering a word. A length Walter stepped forward—then back—viewing Elinor's portrait in various lights, and finally spoke.

"Is there not a change?" said he, in a doubtful and meditative tone. "Yes; the perception of it grows more vivid, the longer I look. It is certainly the same picture that I saw yesterday; the dress—the features—all are the same; and yet something is altered."

"Is, then, the picture less like than it was yesterday?" inquired the painter, now drawing near, with irrepressible interest.

"The features are perfect, Elinor," answered Walter, "and, at the first glance, the expression seemed also hers. But, I could fancy that the portrait has changed countenance while I have been looking at it. The eyes are fixed on mine with a strangely sad and anxious expression. Nay, it is grief and terror! Is this like Elinor?"

"Compare the living face with the pictured one," said the painter.

Walter glanced sidelong at his mistress and started. Motionless and absorbed—fascinated as it were—in contemplation of Walter's portrait, Elinor's face had assumed precisely the expression of which he had just been complaining. Had she practised for whole hours before a mirror, she could not have caught the look so successfully. Had the picture itself been a mirror, it could not have thrown back her present aspect, with stronger and more melancholy truth. She appeared quite unconscious of the dialog between the artist and her lover.

"Elinor," exclaimed Walter, in amazement, "what change has come over you?"

She did not hear him, nor desist from her fixed gaze,

till he seized her hand, and thus attracted her notice; then, with a sudden tremor, she looked from the picture to the face of the original. "Do you see no change in your portrait?" asked she.

"In mine?—None!" replied Walter, examining it. "But let me see! Yes; there is a slight change—an improvement, I think, in the picture, tho none in the likeness. It has a livelier expression than yesterday, as if some bright thoughts were flashing from the eyes, and about to be uttered from the lips. Now that I have caught the look, it becomes very decided."

While he was intent on these observations, Elinor turned to the painter. She regarded him with grief and awe, and felt that he repaid her with sympathy and commiseration, tho wherefore she could but vaguely guess.

"That look!" whispered she, and shuddered. "How came it there?"

"Madam," said the painter, sadly, taking her hand, and leading her apart, "in both these pictures I have painted what I saw. The artist—the true artist—must look beneath the exterior. It is his gift—his proudest but often a melancholy one—to see the inmost soul, and by a power indefinable even to himself to make it glow or darken upon the canvas, in glances that express the thought and sentiment of years. Would that I might convince myself of error in the present instance!"

They had now approached the table, on which were heads in chalk, hands almost as expressive as ordinary faces, ivied church towers, thatched cottages, old thunder-stricken trees, Oriental and antique costume, and all such picturesque vagaries of an artist's idle moments. Turning them over, with seeming carelessness, a crayon sketch of two figures was disclosed.

"If I have failed," continued he, "if your heart does not see itself reflected in your own portrait, if you have no secret cause to trust my delineation of the other, it is not yet too late to alter them. I might change the action of these figures too. But would it influence the event?"

He directed her notice to the sketch. A thrill ran through Elinor's frame; a shriek was upon her lips; but she stifled it, with the self-command that becomes habitual to all who hide thoughts of fear and anguish within their bosoms. Turning from the table, she perceived that Walter had advanced near enough to have seen the sketch, tho she could not determine whether it had caught his eye.

"We will not have the pictures altered," said she hastily. "If mine is sad, I shall but look the gayer for the contrast."

"Be it so," answered the painter, bowing. "May your griefs be such fanciful ones that only your picture may mourn for them! For your joys—may they be true and deep, and paint themselves upon this lovely face till it quite belie my art!"

After the marriage of Walter and Elinor, the pictures formed the two most splendid ornaments of their abode. They hung side by side, separated by a narrow panel, appearing to eye each other constantly, yet always returning the gaze of the spectator. Travelled gentlemen, who professed a knowledge of such subjects, reckoned these among the most admirable specimens of modern portraiture; while common observers compared them with the originals, feature by feature, and were rapturous in praise of the likeness. But it was on a third class—neither travelled connoisseurs nor com-

mon observers, but people of natural sensibility—that
the pictures wrought their strongest effect. Such persons might gaze carelessly at first, but becoming interested, would return day after day, and study these
painted faces like the pages of a mystic volume.
Walter Ludlow's portrait attracted their earliest notice.
In the absence of himself and his bride, they sometimes
disputed as to the expression which the painter had
intended to throw upon the features; all agreeing that
there was a look of earnest import, tho no two
explained it alike. There was less diversity of opinion
in regard to Elinor's picture. They differed, indeed,
in their attempts to estimate the nature and depth of
the gloom that dwelt upon her face, but agreed that it
was gloom, and alien from the natural temperament of
their youthful friend. A certain fanciful person announced, as the result of much scrutiny, that both
these pictures were parts of one design, and that the
melancholy strength of feeling, in Elinor's countenance,
bore reference to the more vivid emotion, or, as he
termed it, the wild passion, in that of Walter. Though
unskilled in the art, he even began a sketch, in which
the action of the two figures was to correspond with
their mutual expression.

It was whispered among friends, that, day by day,
Elinor's face was assuming a deeper shade of pensiveness, which threatened soon to render her too true a
counterpart of her melancholy picture. Walter, on the
other hand, instead of acquiring the vivid look which
the painter had given him on the canvas, became re-
served and downcast, with no outward flashes of emotion, however it might be smouldering within. In
course of time, Elinor hung a gorgeous curtain of
purple silk, wrought with flowers, and fringed with

heavy golden tassels, before the pictures, under pretence that the dust would tarnish their hues, or the light dim them. It was enough. Her visitors felt that the massive folds of the silk must never be withdrawn, nor the portraits mentioned in her presence.

Time wore on; and the painter came again. He had been far enough to the north to see the silver cascade of the Crystal Hills, and to look over the vast round of cloud and forest, from the summit of New England's loftiest mountain. But he did not profane that scene by the mockery of his art. He had also lain in a canoe on the bosom of Lake George, making his soul the mirror of its loveliness and grandeur, till not a picture in the Vatican was more vivid than his recollection. He had gone with the Indian hunters to Niagara, and there, again, had flung his hopeless pencil down the precipice, feeling that he could as soon paint the roar as aught else that goes to make up the wondrous cataract. In truth, it was seldom his impulse to copy natural scenery, except as a framework for the delineations of the human form and face, instinct with thought, passion, or suffering. With store of such, his adventurous ramble had enriched him; the stern dignity of Indian chiefs; the dusky loveliness of Indian girls; the domestic life of wigwams; the stealthy march; the battle beneath gloomy pine trees; the frontier fortress with its garrison; the anomaly of the old French partisan, bred in courts, but grown gray in shaggy deserts; such were the scenes and portraits that he had sketched. The glow of perilous moments; flashes of wild feeling; struggles of fierce power— love, hate, grief, frenzy—in a word, all the worn-out heart of the old earth had been revealed to him under a new form. His portfolio was filled with graphic illustrations of the volume of his memory, which genius would transmute into its own substance, and imbue with immortality. He felt that the deep wisdom in his art, which he had sought so far, was found.

But, amid stern or lovely nature, in the perils of the forest, or its overwhelming peacefulness, still there had been two fantoms, the companions of his way. Like all other men around whom an engrossing purpose wreathes itself, he was insulated from the mass of human kind. He had no aim—no pleasure—no sympathies—but what were ultimately connected with his art. Tho gentle in manner, and upright in intent and action, he did not possess kindly feelings; his heart was cold; no living creature could be brought near enough to keep him warm. For these two beings, however, he had felt, in its greatest intensity, the sort of interest which always allied him to the subjects of his pencil. He had pried into their souls with his keenest insight, and pictured the result upon their features with his utmost skill, so as barely to fall short of that standard which no genius ever reached, his own severe conception. He had caught from the duskiness of the future—at least, so he fancied—a fearful secret, and had obscurely revealed it on the portraits. So much of himself—of his imagination and all other powers—had been lavished on the study of Walter and Elinor, that he almost regarded them as creations of his own, like the thousands with which he had peopled the realms of Picture. Therefore did they flit through the twilight of the woods, hover on the mist of waterfalls, look forth from the mirror of the lake, nor melt away in the noontide sun. They haunted his pictorial fancy, not as mockeries of life, nor pale goblins of the dead, but in the guise of portraits, each with the unalterable expression which his magic had evoked from the caverns of the soul. He could not recross the Atlantic, till he had again beheld the originals of those airy pictures.

"Oh, glorious Art!" thus mused the enthusiastic painter, as he trod the street. "Thou art the image of the Creator's own. The innumerable forms that wander in nothingness start into being at thy beck. The dead live again. Thou recallest them to their old scenes, and givest their gray shadows the luster of a better life, at once earthly and immortal. Thou snatchest back the fleeting moments of History. With thee, there is no Past; for, at thy touch, all that is great becomes forever present; and illustrious men live through long ages, in the visible performance of the very deeds which made them what they are. Oh, potent Art! as thou bringest the faintly revealed Past to stand in that narrow strip of sunlight which we call Now, canst thou summon the shrouded Future to meet her there? Have I not achieved it! Am I not thy Prophet?"

Thus with a proud yet melancholy fervor did he almost cry aloud, as he passed through the toilsome street, among people that knew not of his reveries, nor could understand nor care for them. It is not good for man to cherish a solitary ambition. Unless there be those around him by whose example he may regulate himself, his thoughts, desires, and hopes will become extravagant, and he the semblance, perhaps the reality, of a madman. Reading other bosoms, with an acuteness almost preternatural, the painter failed to see the disorder of his own.

"And this should be the house," said he, looking up and down the front, before he knocked. "Heaven help my brains! That picture! Methinks it will never vanish. Whether I look at the windows or the door, there it is framed within them, painted strongly, and glowing in the richest tints—the faces of the portraits —the figures and actions of the sketch!"

He knocked.

"The portraits! Are they within?" inquired he, of the domestic; then recollecting himself—"your master and mistress! Are they at home?"

"They are, sir," said the servant, adding, as he noticed that picturesque aspect of which the painter could never divest himself, "and the Portraits too!"

The guest was admitted into a parlor, communicating by a central door with an interior room of the same size. As the first apartment was empty, he passed to the entrance of the second, within which his eyes were greeted by those living personages, as well as their pictured representatives, who had long been the object of so singular an interest. He involuntarily paused on the threshold.

They had not perceived his approach. Walter and Elinor were standing before the portraits, whence the former had just flung back the rich and voluminous folds of the silken curtain, holding its golden tassel with one hand, while the other grasped that of his bride. The pictures, concealed for months, gleamed forth again in undiminished splendor, appearing to throw a somber light across the room rather than to be disclosed by a borrowed radiance. That of Elinor had been almost prophetic. A pensiveness, and next a gentle sorrow, had successively dwelt upon her countenance, deepening, with the lapse of time, into a quiet anguish. A mixture of affright would now have made it the very expression of the portrait. Walter's face was moody and dull, or animated only by fitful flashes, which left a heavier darkness for their momentary illumination. He looked from Elinor to her portrait, and thence to his own, in the contemplation of which he finally stood absorbed.

The painter seemed to hear the step of Destiny approaching behind him, on its progress toward its victims. A strange thought darted into his mind. Was not his own the form in which that Destiny had embodied itself, and he a chief agent of the coming evil which he had foreshadowed?

Still, Walter remained silent before the picture, communing with it, as with his own heart, and abandoning himself to the spell of evil influence that the painter had cast upon the features. Gradually his eyes kindled; while, as Elinor watched the increasing wildness of his face, her own assumed a look of terror; and when at last he turned upon her, the resemblance of both to their portraits was complete.

"Our fate is upon us!" howled Walter. "Die!"

Drawing a knife, he sustained her, as she was sinking to the ground, and aimed it at her bosom. In the action and in the look and attitude of each, the painter beheld the figure of his sketch. The picture with all its tremendous coloring was finished.

"Hold, madman!" cried he, sternly.

He had advanced from the door, and interposed himself between the wretched beings, with the same sense of power to regulate their destiny as to alter a scene upon the canvas. He stood like a magician, controlling the fantoms which he had evoked.

"What!" muttered Walter Ludlow, as he relapsed from fierce excitement into silent gloom. "Does Fate impede its own decree?"

"Wretched lady!" said the painter. "Did I not warn you?"

"You did," replied Elinor, calmly, as her terror gave place to the quiet grief which it had disturbed. "But —I loved him!"

Is there not a deep moral in the tale? Could the result of one, or all our deeds, be shadowed forth and set before us—some would call it Fate and hurry onward, others be swept along by their passionate desires—and none be turned aside by the PROPHETIC PICTURES.

"DR. MANETTE'S MANUSCRIPT"

By CHARLES DICKENS

I, Alexander Manette, unfortunate physician, native of Beauvais, and afterwards resident in Paris, write this melancholy paper in my doleful cell in the Bastille, during the last month of the year, 1767. I write it at stolen intervals, under every difficulty. I design to secrete it in the wall of the chimney, where I have slowly and laboriously made a place of concealment for it. Some pitying hand may find it there, when I and my sorrows are dust.

"These words are formed by the rusty iron point with which I write with difficulty in scrapings of soot and charcoal from the chimney, mixed with blood, in the last month of the tenth year of my captivity. Hope has quite departed from my breast. I know from terrible warnings I have noted in myself that my reason will not long remain unimpaired, but I solemnly declare that I am at this time in the possession of my right mind—that my memory is exact and circumstantial—and that I write the truth as I shall answer for these my last recorded words, whether they be ever read by men or not, at the Eternal Judgment-seat.

"One cloudy moonlight night in the third week of December (I think the twenty-second of the month) in the year 1757, I was walking on a retired part of the quay by the Seine for the refreshment of the frosty

114

air, at an hour's distance from my place of residence in the Street of the School of Medicine, when a carriage came along behind me, driven very fast. As I stood aside to let that carriage pass, apprehensive that it might otherwise run me down, a head was put out at the window, and a voice called to the driver to stop.

"The carriage stopped as soon as the driver could rein in his horses, and the same voice called to me by my name. I answered. The carriage was then so far in advance of me that two gentlemen had time to open the door and alight before I came up with it. I observed that they were both wrapped in cloaks, and appeared to conceal themselves. As they stood side by side near the carriage door, I also observed that they both looked of about my own age, or rather younger, and that they were greatly alike, in stature, manner, voice, and (as far as I could see) face too.

" 'You are Doctor Manette?' said one.

" 'I am.'

" 'Doctor Manette, formerly of Beauvais,' said the other; the young physician, originally an expert surgeon, who within the last year or two has made a rising reputation in Paris?'

" 'Gentlemen,' I returned, 'I am that Doctor Manette of whom you speak so graciously.'

" 'We have been to your residence,' said the first, 'and not being so fortunate as to find you there, and being informed that you were probably walking in this direction, we followed, in the hope of overtaking you. Will you please to enter the carriage?'

"The manner of both was imperious, and they both moved, as these words were spoken, so as to place me between themselves and the carriage door. They were armed. I was not.

"'Gentlemen,' said I, 'pardon me; but I usually inquire who does me the honor to seek my assistance, and what is the nature of the case to which I am summoned.'

"The reply to this was made by him who had spoken second. 'Doctor, your clients are people of condition. As to the nature of the case, our confidence in your skill assures us that you will ascertain it for yourself better than we can describe it. Enough. Will you please to enter the carriage?'

"I could do nothing but comply, and I entered it in silence. They both entered after me—the last springing in, after putting up the steps. The carriage turned about, and drove on at its former speed.

"I repeat this conversation exactly as it occurred. I have no doubt that it is, word for word, the same. I describe everything exactly as it took place, constraining my mind not to wander from the task. Where I make the broken marks that follow here, I leave off for the time, and put my paper in its hiding-place. . . .

"The carriage left the streets behind, passed the North Barrier, and emerged upon the country road. At two-thirds of a league from the Barrier—I did not estimate the distance at that time, but afterwards when I traversed it—it struck out of the main avenue, and presently stopped at a solitary house. We all three alighted, and walked, by a damp soft footpath, in a garden where a neglected fountain had overflowed to the door of the house. It was not opened immediately, in answer to the ringing of the bell, and one of my two conductors struck the man who opened it, with his heavy riding glove, across the face.

"There was nothing in this action to attract my particular attention, for I had seen common people struck more commonly than dogs. But the other of the two, being angry likewise, struck the man in like manner with his arm; the look and bearing of the brothers were then so exactly alike that I then first perceived them to be twin brothers.

"From the time of our alighting at the outer gate (which we found locked, and which one of the brothers had opened to admit us, and had relocked), I had heard cries proceeding from an upper chamber. I was conducted to this chamber straight, the cries growing louder as we ascended the stairs, and I found a patient in a high fever of the brain, lying on a bed.

"The patient was a woman of great beauty, and young; assuredly not much past twenty. Her hair was torn and ragged, and her arms were bound to her sides with sashes and handkerchiefs. I noticed that these bonds were all portions of gentleman's dress. On one of them, which was a fringed scarf for a dress of ceremony, I saw the armorial bearings of a Noble, and the letter E.

"I saw this within the first minute of my contemplation of the patient; for, in her restless strivings she had turned over on her face on the edge of the bed, had drawn the end of the scarf into her mouth, and was in danger of suffocation. My first act was to put out my hand to relieve her breathing; and, in moving the scarf aside, the embroidery in the corner caught my sight.

"I turned her gently over, placed my hands upon her breast to calm her and keep her down, and looked into her face. Her eyes were dilated and wild, and she constantly uttered piercing shrieks, and repeated the words, 'My husband, my father, and my brother!' and then counted up to twelve, and said, 'Hush!' For an instant, and no more, she would pause to listen, and then the piercing shrieks would begin again and she would repeat the cry 'My husband, my father, and my brother!' and would count up to twelve, and say, 'Hush!' There was no variation in the order, or the manner. There was no cessation, but the regular moment's pause, in the utterance of these sounds.

" 'How long,' I asked, 'has this lasted?'

"To distinguish the brothers, I will call them the elder and the younger; by the elder, I mean him who exercised the most authority. It was the elder who replied, 'Since about this hour last night.'

" 'She has a husband, a father, and a brother?'

" 'A brother.'

" 'I do not address her brother?'

"He answered with great contempt, 'No.'

" 'She has some recent association with the number twelve?'

"The younger brother impatiently rejoined, 'With twelve o'clock?'

" 'See gentlemen,' said I, still keeping my hands upon her breast, 'how useless I am, as you have brought me! If I had known what I was coming to see, I could have come provided. As it is, time must be lost. There are no medicines to be obtained in this lonely place.'

"The elder brother looked to the younger, who said haughtily, 'There is a case of medicines here;' and brought it from a closet, and put it on the table. . . .

"I opened some of the bottles, smelt them, and put

the stoppers to my lips. If I had wanted to use anything save narcotic medicines that were poisons in themselves, I would not have administered any of those.

"'Do you doubt them?' asked the younger brother.

"'You see, monsieur, I am going to use them,' I replied, and said no more.

"I made the patient swallow, with great difficulty, and after many efforts, the dose that I desired to give. As I intended to repeat it after a while, and as it was necessary to watch its influence, I then sat down by the side of the bed. There was a timid and suppressed woman in attendance (wife of the man down-stairs), who had retreated into a corner. The house was damp and decayed, indifferently furnished—evidently, recently occupied and temporarily used. Some thick old hangings had been nailed up before the windows, to deaden the sound of the shrieks. They continued to be uttered in their regular succession, with the cry, 'My husband, my father, and my brother!' the counting up to twelve, and 'Hush!' The frenzy was so violent, that I had not unfastened the bandages restraining the arms; but I had looked to them, to see that they were not painful. The only spark of encouragement in the case, was, that my hand upon the sufferer's breast had this much soothing influence, that for minutes at a time it tranquillized the figure. It had no effect upon the cries; no pendulum could be more regular.

"For the reason that my hand had this effect (I assume), I had sat by the side of the bed for half an hour, with the two brothers looking on, before the elder said:

"'There is another patient.'

"I was startled, and asked, 'Is it a pressing case?'

" 'You had better see,' he carelessly answered; and took up a light. . . .

"The other patient lay in a back room across a second staircase, which was a species of loft over a stable. There was a low plastered ceiling to a part of it; the rest was open, to the ridge of the tiled roof, and there were beams across. Hay and straw were stored in that portion of the place, fagots for firing, and a heap of apples in sand. I had to pass through that part, to get at the other. My memory is circumstantial and unshaken. I try it with these details, and I see them all, in this my cell in the Bastille, near the close of the tenth year of my captivity, as I saw them all that night.

"On some hay on the ground, with a cushion thrown under his head, lay a handsome peasant boy—a boy of not more than seventeen at the most. He lay on his back, with his teeth set, his right hand clenched on his breast, and his glaring eyes looking straight upward. I could not see where his wound was, as I kneeled on one knee over him; but, I could see that he was dying of a wound from a sharp point.

" 'I am a doctor, my poor fellow,' said I. 'Let me examine it '

" 'I do not want it examined,' he answered; 'let it be.'

"It was under his hand, and I soothed him to let me move his hand away. The wound was a sword-thrust, received from twenty to twenty-four hours before, but no skill could have saved him if it had been looked to without delay. He was then dying fast. As I turned my eyes to the elder brother, I saw him looking down at this handsome boy whose life was ebbing out, as if he were a wounded bird, or hare, or rabbit; not at all as if he were a fellow-creature.

"'How has this been done, monsieur?' said I.

"'A crazed young common dog! A serf! Forced my brother to draw upon him, and has fallen by my brother's sword—like a gentleman.'

"There was no touch of pity, sorrow, or kindred humanity, in this answer. The speaker seemed to acknowledge that it was inconvenient to have that different order of creature dying there, and that it would have been better if he had died in the usual obscure routine of his vermin kind. He was quite incapable of any compassionate feeling about the boy, or about his fate.

"The boy's eyes had slowly moved to him as he had spoken, and they now slowly moved to me.

"'Doctor, they are very proud, these Nobles; but we common dogs are proud too, sometimes. They plunder us, outrage us, beat us, kill us; but we have a little pride left, sometimes. She—have you seen her, Doctor?'

"The shrieks and the cries were audible there, tho subdued by the distance. He referred to them, as if she were lying in our presence.

"I said, 'I have seen her.'

"'She is my sister, Doctor. They have had their shameful rights, these Nobles, in the modesty and virtue of our sisters, many years, but we have had good girls among us. I know it, and have heard my father say so. She was a good girl. She was betrothed to a good young man, too: a tenant of his. We were all tenants of his—that man's who stands there. The other is his brother, the worst of a bad race.'

"It was with the greatest difficulty that the boy gathered bodily force to speak; but, his spirit spoke with a dreadful emphasis.

" 'We were so robbed by that man who stands there, as all we common dogs are by those superior Beings—taxed by him without mercy, obliged to work for him without pay, obliged to grind our corn at his mill, obliged to feed scores of his tame birds on our wretched crops, and forbidden for our lives to keep a single tame bird of our own, pillaged and plundered to that degree that when we chanced to have a bit of meat, we ate it in fear, with the door barred and the shutters closed, that his people should not see it and take it from us—I say, we were so robbed, and hunted, and were made so poor, that our father told us it was a dreadful thing to bring a child into the world, and that what we should most pray for, was, that our women might be barren and our miserable race die out!'

"I had before never seen the sense of being oppressed, bursting forth like a fire. I had supposed that it must be latent in the people somewhere; but, I had never seen it break out, until I saw it in the dying boy.

" 'Nevertheless, Doctor, my sister married. He was ailing at that time, poor fellow, and she married her lover, that she might tend and comfort him in our cottage—our dog-hut, as that man would call it. She had not been married many weeks, when that man's brother saw her and admired her, and asked that man to lend her to him—for what are husbands among us! He was willing enough, but my sister was good and virtuous, and hated his brother with hatred as strong as mine. What did the two then, to persuade her husband to use his influence with her, to make her willing?'

"The boy's eyes, which had been fixed on mine, slowly turned to the looker-on, and I saw in the two faces that all he said was true. The two opposing kinds of pride confronting one another. I can see, even in this Bastille; the gentleman's, all negligent indifference; the peasant's, all trodden-down sentiment, and passionate revenge.

" 'You know, Doctor, that it is among the Rights of these Nobles to harness us common dogs to carts, and drive us. They so harnessed him and drove him. You know that it is among their Rights to keep us in their grounds all night, quieting the frogs, in order that their noble sleep may not be disturbed. They kept him out in the unwholesome mists at night, and ordered him back into harness in the day. But he was not persuaded. No! Taken out of harness one day at noon, to feed—if he could find food—he sobbed twelve times, once for every stroke of the bell, and died on her bosom.'

"Nothing human could have held life in the boy but his determination to tell all his wrong. He forced back the gathering shadows of death, as he forced his clenched right hand to remain clenched, and to cover his wound.

" 'Then, with that man's permission and even with his aid, his brother took her away; in spite of what I know she must have told his brother—and what that is, will not be long unknown to you, Doctor, if it is now—his brother took her away—for his pleasure and diversion, for a little while. I saw her pass me on the road. When I took the tidings home our father's heart burst; he never spoke one of the words that filled it. I took my young sister (for I have another) to a place beyond the reach of this man, and where, at least, she will never be his vassal. Then, I tracked the brother here, and last night climbed in—a common dog, but sword in hand.—where is the loft window? It was somewhere here?'

"The room was darkening to his sight; the world was narrowing around him. I glanced about me, and saw that the hay and straw were trampled over the floor, as if there had been a struggle.

"'She heard me, and ran in. I told her not to come near us till he was dead. He came in and first tossed me some pieces of money; then struck at me with a whip. But I, tho a common dog, so struck at him as to make him draw. Let him break into as many pieces as he will, the sword that he stained with my common blood; he drew to defend himself—thrust at me with all his skill for his life.'

"My glance had fallen, but a few moments before, on the fragments of a broken sword, lying among the hay. That weapon was a gentleman's. In another place, lay an old sword that seemed to have been a soldier's.

"'Now, lift me up, Doctor; lift me up. Where is he?'

"'He is not here,' I said, supporting the body, and thinking that he referred to the brother.

"'He! Proud as these Nobles are, he is afraid to see me. Where is the man who was here? Turn my face to him.'

"I did so, raising the boy's head against my knee. But, invested for the moment with extraordinary power, he raised himself completely: obliging me to rise too, or I could not have still supported him.

"'Marquis,' said the boy, turned to him with his

eyes opened wide, and his right hand raised, 'in the days when all these things are to be answered for, I summon you and yours, to the last of your bad race, to answer for them. I mark this cross of blood upon you, as a sign that I do it. In the days when all these things are to be answered for, I summon your brother, the worst of the bad race, to answer for them separately. I mark this cross of blood upon him; as a sign that I do it.'

"Twice, he put his hand to the wound in his breast, and with his forefinger drew a cross in the air. He stood for an instant with the finger yet raised, and as it dropped, he dropped with it, and I laid him down dead. . . .

"When I returned to the bedside of the young woman, I found her raving in precisely the same order of continuity. I knew that this might last for many hours, and that it would probably end in the silence of the grave.

"I repeated the medicines I had given her, and I sat at the side of the bed until the night was far advanced. She never abated the piercing quality of her shrieks, never stumbled in the distinctness or the order of her words. They were always 'My husband, my father, and my brother! One, two, three, four, five, six, seven, eight, nine, ten, eleven, twelve. Hush!'

"This lasted twenty-six hours from the time when I first saw her. I had come and gone twice, and was again sitting by her, when she began to falter. I did what little could be done to assist that opportunity, and by-and-by she sank into a lethargy, and lay like the dead.

"It was as if the wind and rain had lulled at last, after a long and fearful storm. I released her arms, and called the woman to assist me to compose her figure and the dress she had torn. It was then that I knew her condition to be that of one in whom the first expectations of being a mother have arisen; and it was then that I lost the little hope I had had of her.

" 'Is she dead?' asked the Marquis, whom I will still describe as the elder brother, coming booted into the room from his horse.—'Not dead,' said I; 'but like to die.'

" 'What strength there is in these common bodies!' he said, looking down at her with some curiosity.

" 'There is prodigious strength,' I answered him, 'in sorrow and despair.'

"He first laughed at my words, and then frowned at them. He moved a chair with his foot near to mine, ordered the woman away, and said in a subdued voice:

" 'Doctor, finding my brother in this difficulty with these hinds, I recommended that your aid should be invited. Your reputation is high, and, as a young man with your fortune to make, you are probably mindful of your interest. The things that you see here, are things to be seen, and not spoken of.'

"I listened to the patient's breathing, and avoided answering.—'Do you honor me with your attention, Doctor?'

" 'Monsieur,' said I, 'in my profession, the communications of patients are always received in confidence.' I was guarded in my answer, for I was troubled in my mind with what I had heard and seen.

"Her breathing was so difficult to trace, that I carefully tried the pulse and the heart. There was life, and no more. Looking round as I resumed my seat, I found both the brothers intent upon me. . . .

"I write with so much difficulty, the cold is so

severe, I am so fearful of being detected and consigned to an underground cell and total darkness, that I must abridge this narrative. There is no confusion of failure in my memory; it can recall, and could detail, every word that was ever spoken between me and those brothers.

"She lingered for a week. Towards the last, I could understand some few syllables that she said to me, by placing my ear close to her lips. She asked me where she was, and I told her; who I was, and I told her. It was in vain that I asked her for her family name. She faintly shook her head upon the pillow, and kept her secret, as the boy had done.

"I had no opportunity of asking her any question, until I had told the brothers she was sinking fast, and could not live another day. Until then, tho no one was ever presented to her consciousness save the woman and myself, one or other of them had always jealously sat behind the curtain at the head of the bed when I was there. But when it came to that, they seemed careless what communication I might hold with her; as if—the thought passed through my mind—I were dying too.

"I always observed that their pride bitterly resented the younger brother's (as I call him) having crossed swords with a peasant, and that peasant a boy. The only consideration that appeared to affect the mind of either of them was the consideration that this was highly degrading to the family, and was ridiculous. As often as I caught the younger brother's eyes, their expression reminded me that he disliked me deeply, for knowing what I knew from the boy. He was smoother and more polite to me than the elder; but

I saw this. I also saw that I was an incumbrance in the mind of the elder, too.

"My patient died, two hours before midnight—at a time by my watch, answering almost to the minute when I had first seen her. I was alone with her, when her forlorn young head drooped gently on one side, and all her earthly wrongs and sorrows ended.

"The brothers were waiting in a room down-stairs, impatient to ride away. I had heard them, alone at the bedside, striking their boots with their riding-whips, and loitering up and down.

"'At last she's dead?' said the elder, when I went in.

"'She is dead,' said I.

"'I congratulate you, my brother,' were his words as he turned round.

"He had before offered me money, which I had postponed taking. He now gave me a rouleau of gold. I took it from his hand, but laid it on the table. I had considered the question, and had resolved to accept nothing.

"'Pray excuse me,' said I. 'Under the circumstances, no.'

"They exchanged looks, but bent their heads to me as I bent mine to them, and we parted without another word on either side. . . .

"I am weary, weary, weary—worn down by misery. I cannot read what I have written with this gaunt hand.

"Early in the morning, the rouleau of gold was left at my door in a little box, with my name on the outside. From the first, I had anxiously considered what I ought to do. I decided, that day, to write privately to the Minister, stating the nature of the two cases to which I had been summoned, and the place to which I had gone: in effect, stating all the circumstances. I knew what Court influence was, and what the immunities of the Nobles were, and I expected that the matter would never be heard of; but, I wished to relieve my own mind. I had kept the matter a profound secret even from my wife; and this, too, I resolved to state in my letter. I had no apprehension whatever of my real danger; but I was conscious that there might be danger for others, if others were compromised by possessing the knowledge that I possessed.

"I was much engaged that day, and could not complete my letter that night. I rose long before my usual time next morning to finish it. It was the last day of the year. The letter was lying before me just completed when I was told that a lady waited, who wished to see me. . . .

"I am growing more and more unequal to the task I have set myself. It is so cold, so dark, my senses are so benumbed, and the gloom upon me is so dreadful.

"The lady was young, engaging, and handsome, but not marked for long life. She was in great agitation. She presented herself to me as the wife of the Marquis St. Evrémonde. I connected the title by which the boy had addressed the elder brother, with the initial letter embroidered on the scarf, and had no difficulty in arriving at the conclusion that I had seen that nobleman very lately.

"My memory is still accurate, but I cannot write the words of our conversation. I suspect that I am watched more closely than I was, and I know not at what times I may be watched. She had in part suspected, and in part discovered, the main facts of the cruel story, of her husband's share in it, and my being

resorted to. She did not know that the girl was dead.
Her hope had been, she said in great distress, to show
her, in secret, a woman's sympathy. Her hope had
been to avert the wrath of Heaven from a House that
had long been hateful to the suffering many. She had
reasons for believing that there was a young sister
living, and her greatest desire was, to help that sister.
I could tell her nothing but that there was such a
sister; beyond that, I knew nothing. Her inducement
to come to me, relying on my confidence, had been the
hope that I could tell her the name and place of abode.
Whereas to this wretched hour I am ignorant of
both. . . .

"These scraps of paper fail me. One was taken from
me, with a warning, yesterday. I must finish my
record to-day. She was a good, compassionate lady,
and not happy in her marriage. How could she be!
The brother distrusted and disliked her, and his influence was all opposed to her; she stood in dread of
him, and in dread of her husband too. When I handed
her down to the door, there was a child, a pretty boy
from two to three years old, in her carriage.

" 'For his sake, Doctor,' she said, pointing to him
in tears. 'I would do all I can to make what poor
amends I can. He will never prosper in his inheritance
otherwise. I have a presentiment that if no other innocent atonement is made for this, it will one day be
required of him. What I have left to call my own—
it is little beyond the worth of a few jewels—I wil
make it the first charge of his life to bestow, with the
compassion and lamenting of his dead mother, on thi
injured family, if the sister can be discovered.' Sh
kissed the boy, and said, caressing him, 'It is fo
thine own dear sake. Thou wilt be faithful, littl

Charles?' The child answered her bravely, 'Yes!' I kissed her hand, and she took him in her arms, and went away caressing him. I never saw her more. As she had mentioned her husband's name in the faith that I knew it, I added no mention of it to my letter. I sealed my letter, and, not trusting it out of my own hands, delivered it myself that day.

"That night, the last night of the year, towards nine o'clock, a man in a black dress rang at my gate, demanded to see me, and softly followed my servant, Ernest Defrage, a youth, up-stairs. When my servant came into the room where I sat with my wife—O my wife, beloved of my heart! My fair young English wife!—we saw the man, who was supposed to be at the gate, standing silent behind him.

"'An urgent case in the Rue St. Honoré,' he said. It would not detain me, he had a coach in waiting.

"It brought me here, it brought me to my grave. When I was clear of the house, a black muffler was drawn tightly over my mouth from behind, and my arms were pinioned. The two brothers crossed the road from a dark corner, and identified me with a single gesture. The Marquis took from his pocket the letter I had written, showed it me, burnt it in the light of a lantern that was held, and extinguished the ashes with his foot. Not a word was spoken. I was brought here, I was brought to my living grave.

"If it had pleased God to put it in the hard heart of either of the brothers, in all these frightful years, to grant me any tidings of my dearest wife—so much as to let me know by a word whether alive or dead—I might have thought that He had not quite abandoned them. But, now I believe that the mark of the red cross is fatal to them, and that they have no part in His mercies. And them and their descendants, to the last of their race, I, Alexander Manette, unhappy prisoner, do this last night of the year 1767, in my unbearable agony, denounce to the times when all these things shall be answered for. I denounce them to Heaven and to earth."

THE LAST LESSON

By Alphonse Daudet

I started for school very late that morning and was in great dread of a scolding, especially because M. Hamel had said that he would question us on participles, and I did not know the first word about them. For a moment I thought of running away and spending the day out of doors. It was so warm, so bright! The birds were chirping at the edge of the woods; and in the open field back of the saw-mill the Prussian soldiers were drilling. It was all much more tempting than the rule for participles, but I had the strength to resist, and hurried off to school.

When I passed the town hall there was a crowd in front of the bulletin-board. For the last two years all our bad news had come from there—the lost battles, the draft, the orders of the commanding officer—and I thought to myself, without stopping:

"What can be the matter now?"

Then, as I hurried by as fast as I could go, the blacksmith, Wachter, who was there, with his apprentice, reading the bulletin, called after me:

"Don't go so fast, bub; you'll get to your school in plenty of time!"

I thought he was making fun of me, and reached M. Hamel's little garden all out of breath.

Usually, when school began, there was a great bustle,

which could be heard out in the street, the opening and closing of desks, lessons repeated in unison, very loud, with our hands over our ears to understand better, and the teacher's great ruler rapping on the table. But now it was all so still! I had counted on the commotion to get to my desk without being seen; but, of course, that day everything had to be as quiet as Sunday morning. Through the window I saw my classmates, already in their places, and M. Hamel walking up and down with his terrible iron ruler under his arm. I had to open the door and go in before everybody. You can imagine how I blushed and how frightened I was.

But nothing happened. M. Hamel saw me and said very kindly:

"Go to your place quickly, little Franz. We were beginning without you."

I jumped over the bench and sat down at my desk. Not till then, when I had got a little over my fright, did I see that our teacher had on his beautiful green coat, his frilled shirt, and the little black silk cap, all embroidered, that he never wore except on inspection and prize days. Besides, the whole school seemed so strange and solemn. But the thing that surprised me most was to see, on the back benches that were always empty, the village people sitting quietly like ourselves; old Hauser, with his three-cornered hat, the former mayor, the former postmaster, and several others besides. Everybody looked sad; and Hauser had brought an old primer, thumbed at the edges, and he held it open on his knees with his great spectacles lying across the pages.

While I was wondering about it all, M. Hamel

mounted his chair, and, in the same grave and gentle
tone which he had used to me, said:

"My children, this is the last lesson I shall give you.
The order has come from Berlin to teach only German
in the schools of Alsace and Lorraine. The new master
comes to-morrow. This is your last French lesson. I
want you to be very attentive."

What a thunder-clap these words were to me!

Oh, the wretches; that was what they had put up
at the town-hall!

My last French lesson! Why, I hardly knew how to
write! I should never learn any more! I must stop
there, then! Oh, how sorry I was for not learning
my lessons, for seeking birds' eggs, or going sliding
on the Saar! My books, that had seemed such a
nuisance a while ago, so heavy to carry, my grammar,
and my history of the saints, were old friends now
that I couldn't give up. And M. Hamel, too; the idea
that he was going away, that I should never see him
again, made me forget all about his ruler and how
cranky he was.

Poor man! It was in honor of this last lesson that
he had put on his fine Sunday-clothes, and now I understood why the old men of the village were sitting
there in the back of the room. It was because they
were sorry, too, that they had not gone to school more.
It was their way of thanking our master for his forty
years of faithful service and of showing their respect
for the country that was theirs no more.

While I was thinking of all this, I heard my name
called. It was my turn to recite. What would I not
have given to be able to say that dreadful rule for
the participle all through, very loud and clear, and
without one mistake? But I got mixed up on the first

words and stood there, holding on to my desk, my
heart beating, and not daring to look up. I heard
M. Hamel say to me:

"I won't scold you, little Franz; you must feel bad
enough. See how it is! Every day we have said to
ourselves: 'Bah! I've plenty of time. I'll learn it
to-morrow.' And now you see where we've come out.
Ah, that's the great trouble with Alsace; she puts off
learning till to-morrow. Now those fellows out there
will have the right to say to you: 'How is it; you
pretend to be Frenchmen, and yet you can neither
speak nor write your own language?' But you are not
the worst, poor little Franz. We've all a great deal to
reproach ourselves with.

"Your parents were not anxious enough to have you
learn. They preferred to put you to work on a farm
or at the mills, so as to have a little more money.
And I? I've been to blame also. Have I not often
sent you to water my flowers instead of learning your
lessons? And when I wanted to go fishing, did I not
just give you a holiday?"

Then, from one thing to another, M. Hamel went
on to talk of the French language, saying that it was
the most beautiful language in the world—the clearest,
the most logical; that we must guard it among us and
never forget it, because when a people are enslaved,
as long as they hold fast to their language it is as if
they had the key to their prison. Then he opened a
grammar and read us our lesson. I was amazed to see
how well I understood it. All he said seemed so easy,
so easy! I think, too, that I had never listened so
carefully, and that he had never explained everything
with so much patience. It seemed almost as if the

poor man wanted to give us all he knew before going away, and to put it all into our heads at one stroke.

After the grammar, we had a lesson in writing. That day M. Hamel had new copies for us, written in a beautiful round hand: France, Alsace, France, Alsace. They looked like little flags floating everywhere in the school-room, hung from the rod at the top of our desks. You ought to have seen how every one set to work, and how quiet it was! The only sound was the scratching of the pens over the paper. Once some beetles flew in; but nobody paid any attention to them, not even the littlest ones, who worked right on tracing their fish-hooks, as if that was French, too. On the roof the pigeons cooed very low, and I thought to myself:

"Will they make them sing in German, even the pigeons?"

Whenever I looked up from my writing I saw M. Hamel sitting motionless in his chair and gazing first at one thing, then at another, as if he wanted to fix in his mind just how everything looked in that little school-room. Fancy! For forty years he had been there in the same place, with his garden outside the window and his class in front of him, just like that. Only the desks and benches had been worn smooth; the walnut-trees in the garden were taller, and the hop-vine that he had planted himself twined about the windows to the roof. How it must have broken his heart to leave it all, poor man; to hear his sister moving about in the room above, packing their trunks! For they must leave the country next day.

But he had the courage to hear every lesson to the very last. After the writing, we had a lesson in history, and then the babies chanted their ba, be, bi, bo, bu. Down there at the back of the room old Hauser had put on his spectacles and, holding his primer in both hands, spelled the letters with them. You could see that he, too, was crying; his voice trembled with emotion, and it was so funny to hear him that we all wanted to laugh and cry. Ah, how well I remember it, that last lesson!

All at once the church-clock struck twelve. Then the Angelus. At the same moment the trumpets of the Prussians, returning from drill, sounded under our windows. M. Hamel stood up, very pale, in his chair I never saw him look so tall.

"My friends," said he, "I—I—" But something choked him. He could not go on.

Then he turned to the blackboard, took a piece of chalk, and, bearing on with all his might, he wrote as large as he could:

"Vive La France!"

Then he stopped and leaned his head against the wall, and, without a word, he made a gesture to us with his hand:

"School is dismissed—you may go."

THE MYSTERIOUS MANSION

By Honore De Balzac

About a hundred yards from the town of Vendôme, on the borders of the Loire, there is an old gray house, surmounted by very high gables, and so completely isolated that neither tanyard nor shabby hostelry, such as you may find at the entrance to all small towns, exists in its immediate neighborhood.

In front of this building, overlooking the river, is a garden, where the once well-trimmed box borders that used to define the walks now grow wild as they list. Several willows that spring from the Loire have grown as rapidly as the hedge that encloses it, and half conceal the house. The rich vegetation of those weeds that we call foul adorns the sloping shore. Fruit trees, neglected for the last ten years, no longer yield their harvest, and their shoots form coppices. The wall-fruit grows like hedges against the walls. Paths once graveled are overgrown with moss, but, to tell the truth, there is no trace of a path. From the height of the hill, to which cling the ruins of the old castle of the Dukes of Vendôme, the only spot whence the eye can plunge into this enclosure, it strikes you that, at a time not easy to determine, this plot of land was the delight of a country gentleman, who cultivated roses and tulips and horticulture in general, and who was besides a lover of fine fruit. An arbor is still

visible, or rather the débris of an arbor, where there is
a table that time has not quite destroyed. The aspect
of this garden of bygone days suggests the negative
joys of peaceful, provincial life, as one might recon-
struct the life of a worthy tradesman by reading the
epitaph on his tombstone. As if to complete the sweetness and sadness of the ideas that possess one's soul,
one of the walls displays a sun-dial decorated with the
following commonplace Christian inscription: "Ulti-
mam cogita!" The roof of this house is horribly dilap-
idated, the shutters are always closed, the balconies are
covered with swallows' nests, the doors are perpetually
shut, weeds have drawn green lines in the cracks of
the flights of steps, the locks and bolts are rusty. Sun,
moon, winter, summer, and snow have worn the panel-
ing, warped the boards, gnawed the paint. The lugu-
brious silence which reigns there is only broken by
birds, cats, martins, rats and mice, free to course to
and fro, to fight and to eat each other. Everywhere
an invisible hand has graven the word *mystery*.

Should your curiosity lead you to glance at this
house from the side that points to the road, you would
perceive a great door which the children of the place
have riddled with holes. I afterward heard that this
door had been closed for the last ten years. Through
the holes broken by the boys you would have observed
the perfect harmony that existed between the façades
of both garden and courtyard. In both the same disorder prevails. Tufts of weed encircle the paving-
stones. Enormous cracks furrow the walls, round
whose blackened crests twine the thousand garlands of
the pellitory. The steps are out of joint, the wire of
the bell is rusted, the spouts are cracked. What fire
from heaven has fallen here? What tribunal has

decreed that salt should be strewn on this dwelling? Has God been blasphemed, has France been here betrayed? These are the questions we ask ourselves, but get no answer from the crawling things that haunt the place. The empty and deserted house is a gigantic enigma, of which the key is lost. In bygone times it was a small fief, and bears the name of the Grande Bretêche.

I inferred that I was not the only person to whom my good landlady had communicated the secret of which I was to be the sole recipient, and I prepared to listen.

"Sir," she said, "when the Emperor sent the Spanish prisoners of war and others here, the Government quartered on me a young Spaniard who had been sent to Vendôme on parole. Parole notwithstanding he went out every day to show himself to the sous-préfet. He was a Spanish grandee! Nothing less! His name ended in os and dia, something like Burgos de Férédia. I have his name on my books; you can read it if you like. Oh! but he was a handsome young man for a Spaniard; they are all said to be ugly. He was only five feet and a few inches high, but he was well-grown; he had small hands that he took such care of; ah! you should have seen! He had as many brushes for his hands as a woman for her whole dressing apparatus! He had thick black hair, a fiery eye, his skin was rather bronzed, but I liked the look of it. He wore the finest linen I have ever seen on any one, altho I have had princesses staying here, and, among others, General Bertrand, the Duke and Duchess d'Abrantès, Monsieur Decazes, and the King of Spain. He didn't eat much; but his manners were so polite, so amiable, that one could not owe him a grudge. Oh!

I was very fond of him, altho he didn't open his lips four times in the day, and it was impossible to keep up a conversation with him. For if you spoke to him, he did not answer. It was a fad, a mania with them all, I heard say. He read his breviary like a priest, he went to Mass and to all the services regularly. Where did he sit? Two steps from the chapel of Madame de Merret. As he took his place there the first time he went to church, nobody suspected him of any intention in so doing. Besides, he never raised his eyes from his prayer-book, poor young man! After that, sir, in the evening he would walk on the mountains, among the castle ruins. It was the poor man's only amusement, it reminded him of his country. They say that Spain is all mountains! From the commencement of his imprisonment he stayed out late. I was anxious when I found that he did not come home before midnight; but we got accustomed to this fancy of his. He took the key of the door, and we left off sitting up for him. He lodged in a house of ours in the Rue des Casernes. After that, one of our stablemen told us that in the evening when he led the horses to the water, he thought he had seen the Spanish grandee swimming far down the river like a live fish. When he returned, I told him to take care of the rushes; he appeared vexed to have been seen in the water. At last, one day, or rather one morning, we did not find him in his room; he had not returned. After searching everywhere, I found some writing in the drawer of a table, where there were fifty gold pieces of Spain that are called doubloons and were worth about five thousand francs; and ten thousand francs' worth of diamonds in a small sealed box. The writing said, that in case he did not return, he left us the money and the diamonds, on condition of paying for Masses to thank God for his escape, and for his salvation. In those days my husband had not been taken from me; he hastened to seek him everywhere.

"And now for the strange part of the story. He brought home the Spaniard's clothes, that he had discovered under a big stone, in a sort of pilework by the river-side near the castle, nearly opposite to the Grande Bretêche. My husband had gone there so early that no one had seen him. After reading the letter, he burned the clothes, and according to Count Férédia's desire we declared that he had escaped. The souspréfet sent all the gendarmerie in pursuit of him; but brust! they never caught him. Lepas believed that the Spaniard had drowned himself. I, sir, don't think so; I am more inclined to believe that he had something to do with the affair of Madame de Merret, seeing that Rosalie told me that the crucifix that her mistress thought so much of, that she had it buried with her, was of ebony and silver. Now in the beginning of his stay here, Monsieur de Férédia had one in ebony and silver, that I never saw him with later. Now, sir, don't you consider that I need have no scruples about the Spaniard's fifteen thousand francs, and that I have a right to them?"

"Certainly; but you haven't tried to question Rosalie?" I said.

"Oh, yes, indeed, sir; but to no purpose! the girl's like a wall. She knows something, but it is impossible to get her to talk."

After exchanging a few more words with me, my landlady left me a prey to vague and gloomy thoughts, to a romantic curiosity, and a religious terror not unlike the profound impression produced on us when by night, on entering a dark church, we perceive a faint light under high arches; a vague figure glides by— the rustle of a robe or cassock is heard, and we shudder.

Suddenly the Grande Bretêche and its tall weeds, its barred windows, its rusty ironwork, its closed doors, its deserted apartments, appeared like a fantastic apparition before me. I essayed to penetrate the mysterious dwelling, and to find the knot of its dark story —the drama that had killed three persons. In my eyes Rosalie became the most interesting person in Vendôme. As I studied her, I discovered the traces of secret care, despite the radiant health that shone in her plump countenance. There was in her the germ of remorse or hope; her attitude revealed a secret, like the attitude of a bigot who prays to excess, or of the infanticide who ever hears the last cry of her child. Yet her manners were rough and ingenuous—her silly smile was not that of a criminal, and could you but have seen the great kerchief that encompassed her portly bust, framed and laced in by a lilac and blue cotton gown, you would have dubbed her innocent. No, I thought, I will not leave Vendôme without learning the history of the Grande Bretêche. To gain my ends I will strike up a friendship with Rosalie, if needs be.

"Rosalie," said I, one evening.

"Sir?"

"You are not married?"

She started slightly.

"Oh, I can find plenty of men, when the fancy takes me to be made miserable," she said, laughing.

She soon recovered from the effects of her emotion,

for all women, from the great lady to the maid of the inn, possess a composure that is peculiar to them.

"You are too good-looking and well favored to be short of lovers. But tell me, Rosalie, why did you take service in an inn after leaving Madame de Merret? Did she leave you nothing to live on?"

"Oh, yes! But, sir, my place is the best in all Vendôme."

The reply was one of those that judges and lawyers would call evasive. Rosalie appeared to me to be situated in this romantic history like the square in the midst of a chessboard. She was at the heart of the truth and chief interest; she seemed to me to be bound in the very knot of it. The conquest of Rosalie was no longer to be an ordinary siege—in this girl was centered the last chapter of a novel, therefore from this moment Rosalie became the object of my preference.

One morning I said to Rosalie: "Tell me all you know about Madame de Merret."

"Oh!" she replied in terror, "do not ask that of me, Monsieur Horace."

Her pretty face fell—her clear, bright color faded—and her eyes lost their innocent brightness.

"Well, then," she said, at last, "if you must have it so, I will tell you about it; but promise to keep my secret!"

"Done! my dear girl, I must keep your secret with the honor of a thief, which is the most loyal in the world."

Were I to transcribe Rosalie's diffuse eloquence faithfully, an entire volume would scarcely contain it; so I shall abridge.

The room occupied by Madame de Merret at the Bretêche was on the ground floor. A little closet about four feet deep, built in the thickness of the wall, served as her wardrobe. Three months before the eventful evening of which I am about to speak, Madame de Merret had been so seriously indisposed that her husband had left her to herself in her own apartment, while he occupied another on the first floor. By one of those chances that it is impossible to foresee, he returned home from the club (where he was accustomed to read the papers and discuss politics with the inhabitants of the place) two hours later than usual. His wife supposed him to be at home, in bed and asleep. But the invasion of France had been the subject of a most animated discussion; the billiard-match had been exciting, he had lost forty francs, an enormous sum for Vendôme, where every one hoards, and where manners are restricted within the limits of a praiseworthy modesty, which perhaps is the source of the true happiness that no Parisian covets. For some time past Monsieur de Merret had been satisfied to ask Rosalie if his wife had gone to bed; and on her reply, which was always in the affirmative, had immediately gained his own room with the good temper engendered by habit and confidence. On entering his house, he took it into his head to go and tell his wife of his misadventure, perhaps by way of consolation. At dinner he found Madame de Merret most coquettishly attired. On his way to the club it had occurred to him that his wife was restored to health, and that her convalescence had added to her beauty. He was, as husbands are wont to be, somewhat slow in making this discovery. Instead of calling Rosalie, who was occupied just then in watching the cook and coachman play a difficult hand at brisque, Monsieur de Merret went to his wife's room by the light of a lantern that he deposited on the first step of the staircase. His unmistakable step resounded under the vaulted corridor. At the moment that the Count turned the handle of his wife's door, he fancied he could hear the door of the closet I spoke of close; but when he entered Madame de Merret was alone before the fireplace. The husband thought ingenuously that Rosalie was in the closet, yet a suspicion that jangled in his ear put him on his guard. He looked at his wife and saw in her eyes I know not what wild and hunted expression.

"You are very late," she said. Her habitually pure, sweet voice seemed changed to him.

Monsieur de Merret did not reply, for at that moment Rosalie entered. It was a thunderbolt for him. He strode about the room, passing from one window to the other, with mechanical motion and folded arms.

"Have you heard bad news, or are you unwell?" inquired his wife timidly, while Rosalie undressed her.

He kept silent.

"You can leave me," said Madame de Merret to her maid; "I will put my hair in curl papers myself."

From the expression of her husband's face she foresaw trouble, and wished to be alone with him. When Rosalie had gone, or was supposed to have gone (for she stayed in the corridor for a few minutes), Monsieur de Merret came and stood in front of his wife, and said coldly to her:

"Madame, there is someone in your closet!" She looked calmly at her husband and replied simply:

"No, sir."

This answer was heartrending to Monsieur de Merret; he did not believe in it. Yet his wife had never appeared to him purer or more saintly than at that moment. He rose to open the closet door; Madame de

Merret took his hand, looked at him with an expression of melancholy, and said in a voice that betrayed singular emotion:

"If you find no one there, remember this, all will be over between us!" The extraordinary dignity of his wife's manner restored the Count's profound esteem for her, and inspired him with one of those resolutions that only lack a vaster stage to become immortal.

"No," said he, "Josephine, I will not go there. In either case it would separate us forever. Hear me, I know how pure you are at heart, and that your life is a holy one. You would not commit a mortal sin to save your life."

At these words Madame de Merret turned a haggard gaze upon her husband.

"Here, take your crucifix," he added. "Swear to me before God that there is no one in there; I will believe you, I will never open that door."

Madame de Merret took the crucifix and said:

"I swear."

"Louder," said the husband, "and repeat 'I swear before God that there is no one in that closet.'"

She repeated the sentence calmly.

"That will do," said Monsieur de Merret, coldly.

After a moment of silence:

"I never saw this pretty toy before," he said, examining the ebony crucifix inlaid with silver, and most artistically chiseled.

"I found it at Duvivier's, who bought it of a Spanish monk when the prisoners passed through Vendôme last year."

"Ah!" said Monsieur de Merret, as he replaced the crucifix on the nail, and he rang. Rosalie did not keep him waiting. Monsieur de Merret went quickly to meet her, led her to the bay window that opened on to the garden and whispered to her:

"Listen! I know that Gorenflot wishes to marry you, poverty is the only drawback, and you told him that you would be his wife if he found the means to establish himself as a master mason. Well! go and fetch him, tell him to come here with his trowel and tools. Manage not to awaken any one in his house but himself; his fortune will be more than your desires. Above all, leave this room without babbling, otherwise—" He frowned. Rosalie went away, he recalled her.

"Here, take my latchkey," he said. "Jean!" then cried Monsieur de Merret, in tones of thunder in the corridor. Jean, who was at the same time his coachman and his confidential servant, left his game of cards and came.

"Go to bed, all of you," said his master, signing to him to approach; and the Count added, under his breath: "When they are all asleep—*asleep*, d'ye hear? —you will come down and tell me." Monsieur de Merret, who had not lost sight of his wife all the time he was giving his orders, returned quietly to her at the fireside and began to tell her of the game of billiards and the talk of the club. When Rosalie returned she found Monsieur and Madame de Merret conversing very amicably.

The Count had lately had all the ceilings of his reception rooms on the ground floor repaired. Plaster of Paris is difficult to obtain in Vendôme; the carriage raises its price. The Count had therefore bought a good deal, being well aware that he could find plenty of purchasers for whatever might remain over. This circumstance inspired him with the design he was about to execute.

"Sir, Gorenflot has arrived," said Rosalie in low tones.

"Show him in," replied the Count in loud tones.

Madame de Merret turned rather pale when she saw the mason.

"Gorenflot," said her husband, "go and fetch bricks from the coach-house, and bring sufficient to wall up the door of this closet; you will use the plaster I have over to coat the wall with." Then calling Rosalie and the workman aside:

"Listen, Gorenflot," he said in an undertone, "you will sleep here to-night. But to-morrow you will have a passport to a foreign country, to a town to which I will direct you. I shall give you six thousand francs for your journey. You will stay ten years in that town; if you do not like it, you may establish yourself in another, provided it be in the same country. You will pass through Paris, where you will await me. There I will insure you an additional six thousand francs by contract, which will be paid to you on your return, provided you have fulfilled the conditions of our bargain. This is the price for your absolute silence as to what you are about to do to-night. As to you, Rosalie, I will give you ten thousand francs on the day of your wedding, on condition of your marrying Gorenflot; but if you wish to marry, you must hold your tongues; or—no dowry."

"Rosalie," said Madame de Merret, "do my hair."

The husband walked calmly up and down, watching the door, the mason, and his wife, but without betraying any insulting doubts. Madame de Merret chose a moment when the workman was unloading bricks and

her husband was at the other end of the room to say
to Rosalie: "A thousand francs a year for you, my
child, if you can tell Gorenflot to leave a chink at the
bottom." Then out loud, she added coolly:

"Go and help him!"

Monsieur and Madame de Merret were silent all the
time that Gorenflot took to brick up the door. This
silence, on the part of the husband, who did not choose
to furnish his wife with a pretext for saying things of
a double meaning, had its purpose; on the part of
Madame de Merret it was either pride or prudence.
When the wall was about half-way up, the sly workman took advantage of a moment when the Count's
back was turned, to strike a blow with his trowel in
one of the glass panes of the closet-door. This act
informed Madame de Merret that Rosalie had spoken
to Gorenflot.

All three then saw a man's face; it was dark and
gloomy with black hair and eyes of flame. Before her
husband turned, the poor woman had time to make
a sign to the stranger that signified: Hope!

At four o'clock, toward dawn, for it was the month
of September, the construction was finished. The
mason was handed over to the care of Jean, and Monsieur de Merret went to bed in his wife's room.

On rising the following morning, he said carelessly:

"The deuce! I must go to the Mairie for the passport." He put his hat on his head, advanced three
steps toward the door, altered his mind and took the
crucifix.

His wife trembled for joy. "He is going to Duvivier," she thought. As soon as the Count had left,
Madame de Merret rang for Rosalie; then in a terrible
voice:

"The trowel, the trowel!" she cried, "and quick to work! I saw how Gorenflot did it; we shall have time to make a hole and to mend it again."

In the twinkling of an eye, Rosalie brought a sort of mattock to her mistress, who with unparalleled ardor set about demolishing the wall. She had already knocked out several bricks and was preparing to strike a more decisive blow when she perceived Monsieur de Merret behind her. She fainted.

"Lay Madame on her bed," said the Count coldly. He had foreseen what would happen in his absence and had set a trap for his wife; he had simply written to the mayor, and had sent for Duvivier. The jeweler arrived just as the room had been put in order.

"Duvivier," inquired the Count, "did you buy crucifixes of the Spaniards who passed through here?"

"No, sir."

"That will do, thank you," he said, looking at his wife like a tiger. "Jean," he added, "you will see that my meals are served in the Countess's room; she is ill, and I shall not leave her until she has recovered."

The cruel gentleman stayed with his wife for twenty days. In the beginning, when there were sounds in the walled closet, and Josephine attempted to implore his pity for the dying stranger, he replied, without permitting her to say a word:

"You have sworn on the cross that there is no one there."

THE NECKLACE

By Guy De Maupassant

She was one of those pretty and charming girls who are sometimes, as if by a mistake of destiny, born in a family of clerks. She had no dowry, no expectations, no means of being known, understood, loved, wedded, by any rich and distinguished man; and she let herself be married to a little clerk at the Ministry of Public Instruction.

She dressed plainly because she could not dress well, but she was unhappy as tho she had really fallen from her proper station; since with women there is neither caste nor rank; and beauty, grace, and charm act instead of family and birth. Natural fineness, instinct for what is elegant, suppleness of wit, are the sole hierarchy, and make from women of the people the equals of the very greatest ladies.

She suffered ceaselessly, feeling herself born for all the delicacies and all the luxuries. She suffered from the poverty of her dwelling, from the wretched look of the walls, from the worn-out chairs, from the ugliness of the curtains. All those things, of which another woman of her rank would never even have been conscious, tortured her and made her angry. The sight of the little Breton peasant who did her humble housework aroused in her regrets which were despairing, and distracted dreams. She thought of the silent ante-

(Translated by Jonathan Sturges, and published in "The Odd Number"; copyright, 1889, by Harper & Bros.)

chambers hung with Oriental tapestry, lit by tall bronze candelabra, and of the two great footmen in knee-breeches who sleep in the big armchairs, made drowsy by the heavy warmth of the hot-air stove. She thought of the long *salons* fitted up with ancient silk, of the delicate furniture carrying priceless curiosities, and of the coquettish perfumed boudoirs made for talks at five o'clock with intimate friends, with men famous and sought after, whom all women envy and whose attention they all desire.

When she sat down to dinner, before the round table covered with a table-cloth three days old, opposite her husband, who uncovered the soup tureen and declared with an enchanted air, "Ah, the good *pot-au-feu!* I don't know anything better than that," she thought of dainty dinners, of shining silverware, of tapestry which peopled the walls with ancient personages and with strange birds flying in the midst of a fairy forest; and she thought of delicious dishes served on marvelous plates, and of the whispered gallantries which you listen to with a sphinx-like smile, while you are eating the pink flesh of a trout or the wings of a quail.

She had no dresses, no jewels, nothing. And she loved nothing but that; she felt made for that. She would so have liked to please, to be envied, to be charming, to be sought after.

She had a friend, a former schoolmate at the convent, who was rich, and whom she did not like to go and see any more, because she suffered so much when she came back.

But, one evening, her husband returned home with a triumphant air, and holding, a large envelop in his hand.

"There," said he, "here is something for you."

She tore the paper sharply, and drew out a printed card which bore these words:

"The Minister of Public Instruction and Mme. Georges Ramponneau request the honor of M. and Mme. Loisel's company at the palace of the Ministry on Monday evening, January 18th."

Instead of being delighted, as her husband hoped, she threw the invitation on the table with disdain, murmuring:

"What do you want me to do with that?"

"But, my dear, I thought you would be glad. You never go out, and this is such a fine opportunity. I had awful trouble to get it. Every one wants to go; it is very select, and they are not giving many invitations to clerks. The whole official world will be there."

She looked at him with an irritated eye, and she said, impatiently:

"And what do you want me to put on my back?"

He had not thought of that; he stammered:

"Why, the dress you go to the theater in. It looks very well, to me."

He stopped, distracted, seeing that his wife was crying. Two great tears descended slowly from the corners of her eyes towards the corners of her mouth. He stuttered:

"What's the matter? What's the matter?"

But, by a violent effort, she had conquered her grief, and she replied, with a calm voice, while she wiped her wet cheeks:

"Nothing. Only I have no dress, and therefore I

can't go to this ball. Give your card to some colleague
whose wife is better equipped than I."

He was in despair. He resumed:

"Come, let us see, Mathilde. How much would it
cost, a suitable dress, which you could use on other
occasions, something very simple?"

She reflected several seconds, making her calcula-
tions and wondering also what sum she could ask without drawing on herself an immediate refusal and a
frightened exclamation from the economical clerk.

Finally, she replied, hesitatingly:

"I don't know exactly, but I think I could manage
it with four hundred francs."

He had grown a little pale, because he was laying
aside just that amount to buy a gun and treat himself
to a little shooting next summer on the plain of Nan-
terre, with several friends who went to shoot larks
down there, of a Sunday.

But he said:

"All right. I will give you four hundred francs.
And try to have a pretty dress."

The day of the ball drew near, and Mme. Loisel
seemed sad, uneasy, anxious. Her dress was ready,
however. Her husband said to her one evening:

"What is the matter? Come, you've been so queer
these last three days."

And she answered:

"It annoys me not to have a single jewel, not a single
stone, nothing to put on. I shall look like distress.
I should almost rather not go at all."

He resumed:

"You might wear natural flowers. It's very stylish

at this time of the year. For ten francs you can get two or three magnificent roses."

She was not convinced.

"No; there's nothing more humiliating than to look poor among other women who are rich."

But her husband cried:

"How stupid you are! Go look up your friend Mme. Forestier, and ask her to lend you some jewels. You're quite thick enough with her to do that."

She uttered a cry of joy:

"It's true. I never thought of it."

The next day she went to her friend and told of her distress.

Mme. Forestier went to a wardrobe with a glass door, took out a large jewel-box, brought it back, opened it, and said to Mme. Loisel:

"Choose, my dear."

She saw first of all some bracelets, then a pearl necklace, then a Venetian cross, gold, and precious stones of admirable workmanship. She tried on the ornaments before the glass, hesitated, could not make up her mind to part with them, to give them back. She kept asking:

"Haven't you any more?"

"Why, yes. Look. I don't know what you like."

All of a sudden she discovered, in a black satin box, a superb necklace of diamonds; and her heart began to beat with an immoderate desire. Her hands trembled as she took it. She fastened it around her throat, outside her high-necked dress, and remained lost in ecstasy at the sight of herself.

Then she asked, hesitating, filled with anguish:

"Can you lend me that, only that?"

"Why, yes, certainly."

She sprang upon the neck of her friend, kissed her passionately, then fled with her treasure.

The day of the ball arrived. Mme. Loisel made a great success. She was prettier than them all, elegant, gracious, smiling, and crazy with joy. All the men looked at her, asked her name, endeavored to be introduced. All the attachés of the Cabinet wanted to waltz with her. She was remarked by the minister himself.

She danced with intoxication, with passion, made drunk by pleasure, forgetting all, in the triumph of her beauty, in the glory of her success, in a sort of cloud of happiness composed of all this homage, of all this admiration, of all these awakened desires, and of that sense of complete victory which is so sweet to woman's heart.

She went away about four o'clock in the morning. Her husband had been sleeping since midnight, in a little deserted ante-room, with three other gentlemen whose wives were having a very good time.

He threw over her shoulders the wraps which he had brought, modest wraps of common life, whose poverty contrasted with the elegance of the ball dress. She felt this and wanted to escape so as not to be remarked by the other women, who were enveloping themselves in costly furs.

Loisel held her back.

"Wait a bit. You will catch cold outside. I will go and call a cab."

But she did not listen to him, and rapidly descended the stairs. When they were in the street they did not find a carriage; and they began to look for one, shouting after the cabmen whom they saw passing by at a distance.

They went down towards the Seine, in despair, shivering with cold. At last they found on the quay one of those ancient noctambulant coupés which, exactly as if they were ashamed to show their misery during the day, are never seen round Paris until after nightfall.

It took them to their door in the Rue des Martyrs, and once more, sadly, they climbed up homeward. All was ended for her. And as to him, he reflected that he must be at the Ministry at ten o'clock.

She removed the wraps, which covered her shoulders, before the glass, so as once more to see herself in all her glory. But suddenly she uttered a cry. She had no longer the necklace around her neck!

Her husband, already half-undressed, demanded:

"What is the matter with you?"

She turned madly towards him:

"I have—I have—I've lost Mme. Forestier's necklace."

He stood up, distracted.

"What!—how?—Impossible!"

And they looked in the folds of her dress, in the folds of her cloak, in her pockets, everywhere. They did not find it.

He asked:

"You're sure you had it on when you left the ball?"

"Yes, I felt it in the vestibule of the palace."

"But if you had lost it in the street we should have heard it fall. It must be in the cab."

"Yes. Probably. Did you take his number?"

"No. And you, didn't you notice it?"

"No."

They looked, thunderstruck, at one another. At last Loisel put on his clothes.

"I shall go back on foot," said he, "over the whole route which we have taken, to see if I can't find it."

And he went out. She sat waiting on a chair in her ball dress, without strength to go to bed, overwhelmed, without fire, without a thought.

Her husband came back about seven o'clock. He had found nothing.

He went to Police Headquarters, to the newspaper offices, to offer a reward; he went to the cab companies—everywhere, in fact, whither he was urged by the least suspicion of hope.

She waited all day, in the same condition of mad fear before this terrible calamity.

Loisel returned at night with a hollow, pale face; he had discovered nothing.

"You must write to your friend," said he, "that you have broken the clasp of her necklace and that you are having it mended. That will give us time to turn round."

She wrote at his dictation.

At the end of a week they had lost all hope.

And Loisel, who had aged five years, declared:

"We must consider how to replace that ornament."

The next day they took the box which had contained it, and they went to the jeweler whose name was found within. He consulted his books.

"It was not I, madame, who sold that necklace; I must simply have furnished the case."

Then they went from jeweler to jeweler, searching for a necklace like the other, consulting their memories, sick both of them with chagrin and with anguish.

They found, in a shop at the Palais Royal, a string of diamonds which seemed to them exactly like the

one they looked for. It was worth forty thousand
francs. They could have it for thirty-six.

So they begged the jeweler not to sell it for three
days yet. And they made a bargain that he should
buy it back for thirty-four thousand francs, in case
they found the other one before the end of February.

Loisel possessed eighteen thousand francs which his
father had left him. He would borrow the rest.

He did borrow, asking a thousand francs of one,
five hundred of another, five louis here, three louis
there. He gave notes, took up ruinous obligations,
dealt with usurers, and all the race of lenders. He
compromised all the rest of his life, risked his signa-
ture without even knowing if he could meet it; and,
frightened by the pains yet to come, by the black misery which was about to fall upon him, by the prospect
of all the physical privations and of all the moral tor-
tures which he was to suffer, he went to get the new
necklace, putting down upon the merchant's counter
thirty-six thousand francs.

When Mme. Loisel took back the necklace Mme.
Forestier said to her, with a chilly manner:

"You should have returned it sooner, I might have
needed it."

She did not open the case, as her friend had so much
feared. If she had detected the substitution, what
would she have thought, what would she have said?
Would she not have taken Mme. Loisel for a thief?

Mme. Loisel now knew the horrible existence of the
needy. She took her part, moreover, all on a sudden,
with heroism. That dreadful debt must be paid. She
would pay it. They dismissed their servant; they
changed their lodgings; they rented a garret under the
roof.

She came to know what heavy housework meant and the odious cares of the kitchen. She washed the dishes, using her rosy nails on the greasy pots and pans. She washed the dirty linen, the shirts, and the dish-cloths, which she dried upon a line; she carried the slops down to the street every morning, and carried up the water, stopping for breath at every landing. And, dressed like a woman of the people, she went to the fruiterer, the grocer, the butcher, her basket on her arm, bargaining, insulted, defending her miserable money sou by sou.

Each month they had to meet some notes, renew others, obtain more time.

Her husband worked in the evening making a fair copy of some tradesman's accounts, and late at night he often copied manuscript for five sous a page.

And this life lasted ten years.

At the end of ten years they had paid everything, everything, with the rates of usury, and the accumulations of the compound interest.

Mme. Loisel looked old now. She had become the woman of impoverished households—strong and hard and rough. With frowsy hair, skirts askew, and red hands, she talked loud while washing the floor with great swishes of water. But sometimes, when her husband was at the office, she sat down near the window, and she thought of that gay evening of long ago, of that ball where she had been so beautiful and so fêted.

What would have happened if she had not lost that necklace? Who knows? who knows? How life is strange and how changeful! How little a thing is needed for us to be lost or to be saved!

But, one Sunday, having gone to take a walk in the

Champs Elysées to refresh herself from the labors of the week, she suddenly perceived a woman who was leading a child. It was Mme. Forestier, still young, still beautiful, still charming.

Mme. Loisel felt moved. Was she going to speak to her? Yes, certainly. And now that she had paid, she was going to tell her all about it. Why not?

She went up.

"Good-day, Jeanne."

The other, astonished to be familiarly addressed by this plain goodwife, did not recognize her at all, and stammered:

"But—madame!—I do not know— You must have mistaken."

"No. I am Mathilde Loisel."

Her friend uttered a cry.

"Oh, my poor Mathilde! How you are changed!"

"Yes, I have had days hard enough, since I have seen you, days wretched enough—and that because of you!"

"Of me! How so?"

"Do you remember that diamond necklace which you lent me to wear at the ministerial ball?"

"Yes. Well?"

"Well, I lost it."

"What do you mean? You brought it back."

"I brought you back another just like it. And for this we have been ten years paying. You can understand that it was not easy for us, us who had nothing. At last it is ended, and I am very glad."

Mme. Forestier had stopped.

"You say that you bought a necklace of diamonds to replace mine?"

"Yes. You never noticed it, then! They were very like."

And she smiled with a joy which was proud and naïve at once.

Mme. Forestier, strongly moved, took her two hands.

"Oh, my poor Mathilde! Why, my necklace was paste. It was worth at most five hundred francs!"